by Terrence Lore Smith

THE DEVIL AND WEBSTER DANIELS
THE THIEF WHO CAME TO DINNER

The Devil and Webster Daniels

The Devil and Webster Daniels

TERRENCE LORE SMITH

Red Wing Public Library
Red Wing, MN 55066

PUBLISHED FOR THE CRIME CLUB BY
DOUBLEDAY & COMPANY, INC.
GARDEN CITY, NEW YORK
1975

All of the characters in this book are fictitious, and any resemblance to actual persons, living or dead, is purely coincidental.

Library of Congress Cataloging in Publication Data
Smith, Terrence Lore.
The devil and Webster Daniels.
I. Title.
PZ4.S6588De [PS3569.M538] 813'.5'4
ISBN 0-385-00321-8
Library of Congress Catalog Card Number 74-25125

Copyright © 1975 by Terrence L. Smith
All Rights Reserved
Printed in the United States of America
First Edition

For Warren and Richmond: With great affection for two truly fine gentlemen, friends, human fellows.

Acknowledgments:

Once again, to family and friends for encouragement and support; most especially to David Doman for suggesting that Laura and Webster deserved another novel.

More devils can be routed by a little laughter than by a carload of humorless piety.
    —*Charles Merrill Smith*

Reprinted from *The New York Times Review of Books*, of Sunday, October 26, 1975:

WORTHY OVERSELL *Diamonds Are a Boy's Best*
by Oliver Longly-Bain *Friend*, by Webster Daniels
(Author's House, 341 pps., $10.00)

One hardly knows where to begin with a book like this. How do you cut through the hoopla and frantic flack of a prepackaged best seller? Its initial printing was a quarter of a million copies and advance sale, reportedly, is already half that figure; with its pub date only a month past it is already listed as the number one best seller in the country; for months, zealous press agents have been heralding its publication as if the angel Gabriel were preparing to blow in the judgment day; astronomical sums have been prepaid for first serial rights (*Playboy*), book clubs (five of them), motion picture rights (Warner Brothers), and foreign rights (twenty-two countries). It is said that the author has already pocketed nearly a million dollars, and the paperback rights auction, which will be held later this month, is expected to bring that much again, at least.

The best approach is to try to look at the thing itself without the filters and distortions supplied for us. Happily, this is one of the rare occasions when the blockbuster is worthy of its success.

For those few who lead simple, unaware lives far from the madding media, the book is the memoirs of the Chess Burglar, who was something of a national diversion in the late sixties with his dramatic and arrogant superthefts of

The Devil and Webster Daniels

jewels in Chicago. The book, as the boys say, tells all. Mr. Daniels ably and wittily chronicles his all-American-boy youth, the dissolution of his marriage after he had worked hard to achieve one of the more common versions of the American dream, his disillusionment with the boredom and hypocrisy of the business world, his turn to spectacular and successful crime, his aggrandizement of a beautiful and wealthy young woman (Laura Deveraux) as both lover and cocriminal, his battle of wits and wills with an alert insurance investigator who became something of a classic adversary for him, his celebrated chess game with a Chicago chess columnist for which he left moves at the scenes of his crimes, and his triumphal exit to Europe with the proceeds of his crimes safely hoarded in a Swiss bank. That storybook adventure tale makes this autobiography better reading than most thriller novels and, if that were all to the book, it would be well worthy of the reading.

However, Mr. Daniels gives us more. He shows us the piece-by-piece development of a personal philosophy which embraces a morality in antisocial acts. It won't be your morality (nor is it mine), but he makes a telling case that the most widely practiced and most serious immorality of our time is the abdication of individual conscience to other moral authority. He believes that to abdicate conscience to church, school, corporation, society, or nation is the very center of modern man's seeming alienation and loss of humanity. He gives us no solutions other than the maxim that each individual must accept responsibility for his acts. "The soldier is not justified in pulling the trigger unless he, personally, believes in the justness of the war."

So seeing a vastly corrupt society around him, he decided to turn from white-collar theft to workingman burglary. This accomplished the dual purpose of endangering himself—making himself accountable, responsible—and jabbing society's smugness and hypocrisy. Since the statute of limitations has expired, he is not endangered by his "confession," but he, rightly, notes he faces the moral outrage of governments and their great capacity for harassment. You may not agree with him, but he is a singular man with an intelligent and incisive argument.

As if all this were not enough, the book is handsomely packaged with thirty or so excellent photographs. I have no doubt it will become the cocktail-table book of the decade and one that you needn't curl your lip at to maintain self-respect.

The Devil and Webster Daniels

CHAPTER I

Devil's Advocate

Don Cravat, prime-time Puck of talk-show television, spins his chair, turns his sandy hair, boyish face toward Webster. Notice how his cheeks hollow when he's thinking, Webster; makes him look hungry; carnivore.

"But, Mr. Daniels, isn't there a law against profiting from your crime? Wouldn't your royalties from this book make you liable for prosecution under that law?" Smirks.

"There is such a law. Whether or not it would apply in my case, I don't know. I've never been convicted of any crime. It seems to me that would be a prerequisite. But the point is moot. I'm not profiting monetarily from the book. All my, after taxes, royalties have been assigned to Amnesty, Inter-

national, an organization which works for the humane treatment and/or release of political prisoners around the world."
Webster squirms; hot studio lights?; whiff of hostility in the questions?; commercial virtue, Webster?

"Very decent of you, I'm sure." Puck pouting?

"Yes, I think so." Smug, Webster?

After a commercial break, the camera comes to Cravat again. He holds up a copy of Webster's book.

"For those of you who have just joined us, we are talking with Webster Daniels, author of the publishing sensation of the year—*Diamonds Are a Boy's Best Friend*, his account of his escapades as the notorious Chess Burglar. Also with us are Laura Deveraux, his partner in crime and love; Bobbie Deams, his go-between; Dave Reilly, the insurance investigator who pursued the case; and Lina Sarazen, the well-known actress who is presently Dave's wife and formerly, Mrs. Webster Daniels." He sets the book aside. Turns to Bobbie Deams. "What was the greatest difficulty you had in fencing the stolen jewels?"

Bobbie, the hardnosed brawler, two-fisted drinker, a little portly now, mellow. "After the hit at the Art Institute, when Webster took the Jellane jewels, he and Laura flew them over in her seaplane and the meet was set up off the Spanish coast from Cartagena. We wanted a portfolio of bonds instead of cash, so I had to go with the man while he got them and then stay with him for two days until the meet. I couldn't take a chance on him making a switch and giving us fake bonds. So I didn't sleep for two days."

"How much money did you make as Webster's go-between?"

"Something over a million dollars."

"So crime does pay, after all." Puck, with a sly-rabbit grin. "How much did you make, Webster?"

"Before or after business expenses and splits?" Webster

grinning. "Just like any other entrepreneur, I found that enterprise is seldom free."

"Profit, then."

"Something over three million dollars." Webster's eyes are shining. "I like to think I'm the most successful thief of the second-story type around."

Cravat laughs. "Is there a formula to determine it? How much weight to give to length of career versus financial gain?"

"Yes, I suppose we'd have to have a computer to figure it. Certainly it seems I should get very high marks for zero days in the slammer."

Cravat smiles, turns to Dave; tanned, looks good, healthy, perhaps younger than he did seven years ago; ulcers gone? "I'm fascinated, Mr. Reilly, by the fact that, after pursuing Webster so doggedly, you didn't turn him in when you caught him in the act."

"Webster would call it a perfect union of form and content. Art. He had jarred my thinking with his philosophy enough so that I couldn't attack him. I don't say that he converted me, but I was no longer absolutely sure of my viewpoint." Dave shrugs. "I didn't want the responsibility of smashing his life on my head."

"Do you think it's right that a confessed criminal is free on a legal technicality and is being made into a celebrity?"

Dave smiles. "Let Webster answer that one. He says it better than I do."

"Well then, Mr. Daniels?" Puck tries to pin you with straight gaze and raised brow, Webster.

Now Webster smirks. "But, my dear boy, of course it is. If laws aren't faithfully executed, and they aren't, that only makes the law more absurd than it naturally is. Technicality? That is all the law is. A technique. You are confusing justice with law and they are never the same. As for making me a celebrity, I suppose I'm as worthy a candidate for that dubious honor as a football player or a gossip columnist. Since it's all rather whimsical I don't see that it matters much."

After a while the show is over. Cravat does not thank them for coming, but the producer does. Perhaps, you pricked Puck's ego, Webster; Puck pissed?

The five have a few drinks in a bar nearby and reminisce. Late-night Manhattan; everything is filthy and the only look people have is a dull hostility; the neon is as cheap as the beads the Indians took; it was probably a nice little island then. Anxious to get back to Europe, Webster?

"We'll be in the city for a while. Lina's got to start rehearsal for her musical and there's a chance of a movie role for me in a picture shooting here."

"We'll have to get together again. Go out for dinner." Dave and Lina make agreeable sounds; Laura looks funny at Lina. "When are you taking off, Bobbie?"

"I have to stick around for a month or so. Business."

"Business? I thought you retired on our ill-gotten gains, Bobbie."

"Another kind of business."

"Wouldn't have anything to do with that CIA man that tried to recruit you in Amsterdam?"

Looks evasive, Webster. "Not directly."

Later, Laura and Webster taxi back to the hotel; the Stanhope—small, quiet, a view of the park and the Met; in the room, disrobe.

Webster stares in the mirror. The tall frame is no longer rangy; a hint of jowls and a small paunch; thirty-nine and too much loafing, Webster. You don't do much any more. Eat, sleep, party, sun yourself on the Riviera. Yawn.

Laura lies beside him on the bed. "Is that the last one of those things?"

Devil's Advocate

"That's what the schedule says."

"Thank God."

"I don't believe he's connected with my publisher."

"Well, whoever. A month of TV and press interviews and autographing parties and literary luncheons is enough."

"A superfluity."

"Yes. It was nice to see Dave and Bobbie and, uh, Lina."

"They all looked great, didn't they?"

"Yes . . . of course. . . ."

Webster eyes Laura. "I don't think I'm going to like this at all."

She shrugs. "Then you don't have to listen."

Webster sighs. "That will be worse. What was it?"

"Nothing." She lights a cigarette and turns her back.

"Let's see. Mmmm, something about that frightfully tacky little smock Lina was wearing? Doesn't do a thing for her? With her coloring, she shouldn't try to wear turquoise? Something like that?"

Laura erupts from the bed and walks wordlessly into the bathroom. Shuts the door. Forcefully.

Some time passes. Webster lights a cigarette. Picks up a copy of his book. Appraises the dust jacket, his photograph for the nth time. Author's pride. And no ghost-writing.

Laura peeks out the bathroom door. Wistful, repentant. "Sorry." He smiles and shakes his head and she comes to him, her dark hair golden long form jade-green eyes still-high breasts and molds herself to him. Mouths meet. And then, "I was being bitchy, wasn't I?"

"You were about to be."

"Well, now I'm being sexy."

Webster nods. "You're about to be."

They come together in the hot of love; freely given, freely received.

The Devil and Webster Daniels

After, with the lights out, she asks, "What's wrong with us lately, Webster?"
"Not that."
"No. But I'm bitchy and you're . . . what?"
"Bored is the word. I guess we miss the excitement."
"And we don't do much."
"Yes."
"We'll have to think of something, Webster."
"Yes."

    Barbra Streisand; "The Way We Were."

CHAPTER II

Devil's Disciple

Chill fall eve. Webster in red crushed-velvet tux, Laura in metallic-green evening sheath; sidewalk standers; cab seekers.
"There's one."
"Where?"
"Over there."
"Where is over there?"
"Never mind, it's gone."
Webster slumps shoulders. "I don't see why we can't skip this party. Why don't you call them and tell them we couldn't find a taxi?"
"Vera Sloan is my roommate from college and we can't let her down."

The Devil and Webster Daniels

"Mmmmpphh."

"If you weren't quite so well fortified with scotch, you'd be able to get a cab."

"Why? Hackies have something against drinkers?"

"Webster!"

"If I wasn't so well fortified, I probably wouldn't be able to stand this party."

"Webster!"

"I'll get a cab. I'll get a cab."

Taxi riders; surly hackie; silent passage. Gramercy Park townhouse; converted brownstone; butler at the door, guests inside.

Caulder and Vera Sloan are beautiful people; he graying mod hair stylish lean forties and inherited wealth—the best kind; dabbles in the arts, backs films and plays, owns a vineyard; she red haired voluptuous just shy of plump Rita Hayworth mid-thirties and tired or worried; makes the society columns, jet sets.

"Dear Laura, so wonderful of you to come and Webster, darling, so many of our guests are so anxious to meet you." Shoot Laura a glance, Webster, and get a raised brow; grin and bear it.

Rod Rex, the movie critic who looks like a star, "I really hope, Mr. Daniels, you're not going to let them ruin that lovely story of yours. If they do it right, it could be the moviest movie of the decade."

"They haven't really asked me for suggestions, after I suggested myself for the lead. I'm afraid they weren't amused."

"The studio people are frightfully devoid of a sense of humor. They only make comedy by accident now."

Lymon Capon, the tiny novelist, "As I was saying to my dear friend, Jackie, the other day, isn't it a tragedy what chic has come to in our time? Imagine that dreadfully earthy Redford person as the most glamorous star! Tacky, tacky,

Devil's Disciple

tacky!" Forgive him his posture, Webster, for he writes so beautifully.

Malvina Boonsoon, model, actress, *Time* magazine cover girl glamor beauty. "I admire you so, Webster; you live so dramatically, so freely. We have so little time we must seize it, live deeply, freely, frantically. Real life ends at thirty-five, don't you think?"

"Well, actually, no. I'm thirty-nine now."

She looks deeply and soulfully into your eyes as she cups your face with long graceful fingers. "Oh, you poor brave beautiful man. How you must suffer."

"No, actually, if you keep a decent buzz on, the conversation doesn't bother you nearly as much. And the scotch is very good."

Sucks in her breath. "So brave!"

Moorman Naillor, the heavyweight champion bourbon drinker of the *literati*. "Pretty good stuff, Daniels. Real adventure, danger. Live it, then write it." Shakes his head admiringly. "The kind of thing Papa would have been really proud of."

"That's a relief. I've always been worried about my masculinity."

"Really?"

"Sure. When I played tight end for Northwestern it was good. The clean feel of the defensive end clawing your face and clubbing your head, the sharp sweet tone of your metal cup from a ringing knee to the groin, the heady feel of a hard hit downfield, and the sound of your man's kneecap popping and shattering. It was good. But I didn't make all-American, because my woman was a castrating bitch. She kept trying to compete with me. We'd be walking along the street and she'd throw a rolling block at a group of strangers. The hospital bills and lawsuits were terrible. I became depressed and ineffectual. And there just isn't the same virility to being all big ten as all-American. So I've wondered if I should have beat her into line ever since. I could have gotten one of my teammates and done a little x and y crisscross two-on-one blocking on the broad. Straightened her out in a hurry. I've always felt less of a man for it." He has passed out, Webster; snores on the floor; another beautiful writer with a weird mind and certain stupidities.

Mingle with the other guests. More beautiful people. Forty or fifty of them. Wasn't that a dream you had once, Webster? Wasn't that why you had the hair graft to cover your balding head, the nose job to straighten the football breaks, teeth capped, and acquired the tan to cover the football scars? Oh, well, Webster, the scotch *is* good and if you keep moving around the large living room and terraces, nimbly avoiding the hard-edged Swedish-modern furniture and *objets d'art*, you can avoid being hemmed in.

People tell Webster more than he really wants to know about how dreary the season was on Majorca last year, the advantages of tax-free municipals (if you're in the 70 per cent bracket and who isn't?), how awfully commercial Andy Warhol has gotten, and who is *really* in, who is *really* out.

Later Laura mercifully motions him across the room, down a corridor.

"Can we leave?"

"Soon, love. First, Vera wants to talk to us. She's very upset."

"I don't blame her. I've met her friends."

"Webster, you are being positively snotty tonight. My God, I know those people are crashing bores and most of them are more or less useless, but what makes us so much better?"

"I was hoping you wouldn't ask that. At least we don't take ourselves so seriously."

"Is that enough?"

Devil's Disciple

"Probably not."

Up a flight of stairs and down a second corridor, they enter a gigantic bedroom with mirror walls and silver appointments. Vera is sitting somewhat slumped on a silver satin couch across the room. Several of you crossing the room everywhere you look, Webster; Narcissus. Webster sits in a close easy chair, crosses his legs, sips his scotch. Laura sits by Vera on the couch. She looks from one to the other like a small child in need of some reassurance, approval.

"There was something you wanted to ask me, Vera."

"Yes, Webster. There is." She is kneading her hands and the skin is beginning to get red marks. "I hate to tell this to you."

Webster frowns. "Then maybe you shouldn't. We're not going to judge you, Vera. You should know that, but if it makes you too uncomfortable to share the . . . whatever . . ."

She shakes her head. "No, I have to. I haven't anywhere else to turn." She stares awhile and sighs. Finally, "I'm being blackmailed. I . . . I suppose you'll have to know what about."

"Before you give us the details, maybe you'd better specify what kind of help you're going to ask for."

"I want you . . . I was hoping you could, you would get some . . . things for me."

"Steal them?"

"Yes."

"That's not very feasible. I won't say I'm on the mind of every cop in the country, but my, er, exploits and the publicity from this book don't make me a likely candidate for the PBA's Man of the Year Award. Some of them are so unkind as to suggest that I ought to be imprisoned. I'm retired and this book pretty well makes it permanent."

"But he couldn't go to the police; he's a blackmailer, and

The Devil and Webster Daniels

besides, he doesn't live in New York City. He lives in Putnam County and you're not known up there."

"Who is this Putnam County blackmailer?"

"The devil."

They stare. Webster throws back his head and laughs. "Pardon me. I always wondered where he lived. I never thought of Putnam County. Does he commute?"

"Webster, don't."

"I didn't start the gag."

"It's not a joke. I thought he was just a witch at first, but now I feel . . . I almost feel he's the devil."

Webster sighs, sips scotch. "I guess you'll have to tell us all about it."

Vera nods. "His name is Edward Allenby. I met him through some friends while I was staying at our country place near Brewster. He is terribly attractive. Tall and dark and . . . rather magnetic, exciting. At first I just thought it was going to be one of those exciting diversions one has from time to time. Caulder has a few and I have, but we always manage them so they don't interfere with our lives. We don't speak about it, but it's . . . well, it's understood. I hate to sound so cheap. . . ."

Laura pats her hand. "We understand, Vera. Don't worry about us."

Webster nods, stifles a yawn. "We don't expect other people to judge our morality, Vera. God knows we wouldn't pay any attention if they did." He shrugs. "We won't judge you either."

"Well, I guess I began to be rather . . . mad about him. I lost my head completely. I even thought of leaving Caulder and the children, though that wasn't very serious and it certainly wasn't what Edward wanted. He's very artful at drawing you in and slowly chopping away your options. After two months, he brought me into the coven. He had hinted

Devil's Disciple

at it before, but I guess he waits until he thinks he has you under control. Thinks! Knows. He had to know I would do anything for him at that point. And . . . and . . . where was I?"

"The coven."

"Yes. The coven. I was the thirteenth initiate, making a complete coven. Thirteen women. All rather like myself. It seemed exciting at first and, of course, witchcraft is rather the thing now. We had regular Sabbats and black masses and the, uh, well, you know . . . the group thing, group-sex thing." She reddens; looks excessive with her coloring, Webster. "It sounds so terribly awful, just telling it, I know, but at the time it seemed exciting and very liberated. Then it became shabby when he told me he had films and wanted money. Since then it has become very sinister."

"Why?"

"It isn't just the money now. He makes me keep coming to the, uh, meetings. It's more than money to him. He wants some sort of power over me. He has power, but I feel he wants more. It's almost as if he wants to use me, to reach through me, to get at something larger. I really don't know what, but it's a feeling I have. It's what almost makes me feel as if he's the devil. I know that sounds foolish, but if you knew him . . ."

"If Caulder is as, er, tolerant as you say, why don't you just tell him? Why submit?"

"I would, but for the films. I won't say Caulder isn't tolerant, but the films are . . . very vivid. They would make an impression that would be very hard to forget. If it were just my word against his, Caulder wouldn't listen to him and couldn't use . . . this. Legally."

"What makes you think he would want to use it legally? Has he talked about a divorce? For some other reason?"

"Not exactly, but he does have a particularly attractive

diversion of his own at the moment and sometimes he talks vaguely about freedom, his freedom. I know it must not sound like it, but I really love Caulder and our children. I don't want to lose my home and family."

"You made a hell of a mess playing those games." Webster sighs.

"Webster!"

"Okay, Laura." Webster stands up, paces. There is a certain appeal, Webster. The challenge and the being back in it. "How much is he bleeding you for?"

"Twenty-five hundred a month."

"Presumably, he's victimizing the others as well? The other members of the coven?"

"Yes."

"Almost four hundred thousand a year. How long has this been going on?"

"Six months."

Multiples of Webster pace; the mirror images in motion are disturbing, Webster; reflections of reflective man. "I don't like it. I'm not an amateur; I'm a professional. Not to be immodest, but I am probably the greatest living thief. I steal for money. Among other things."

"If it's a question of money, I can pay. My God, I am paying. How much do you want?"

"I don't need money. I don't want your money. I have more money than I'll ever spend. That's why I retired."

Vera sags; wilted woman. "Then you won't help?"

"Webster, why can't she pay a fee for this to Amnesty, International? Then it would still be professional."

"I could do that, Webster. I could pay whatever you say. A hundred thousand dollars. I would pay that much to get those films."

You're hooked, Webster; no point in frowning at Laura;

Devil's Disciple

no graceful way out and you pride yourself on style. Don't you really want to anyway? Webster sighs.

"I suppose you'd better tell me all about this man—where he lives, how I can get to him, all of it. You'll have to help."

"Anything. I'll do anything."

Webster suppresses the comment that that was the trouble in the first place; sit down and listen. Laura doesn't suppress a smile. Vera has come to life; sees hope.

And back at the hotel, Laura can't quite understand why the excitement is soured. It just seems too *nice* a thing to do, Webster? The potential for self-righteousness is too high? Relax, you've cut it with this crowd before.

Ramsey Lewis Trio; "The In Crowd."

CHAPTER III

Devil's Adversaries

Morning in Putnam County, New York. Webster on the move; sweat shirt, sweat pants, sweat socks, sneakers; sweat. Webster runs. A cool fall sun shines. The grass is still green, but the leaves are turning or turned. The Sloan estate; nine point seven acres, wooded and rolling, fishpond, large landscaped lawn, swimming pool, tennis courts, nine-car garage, nine cars, twenty-four-room stone mansion, three five-room Mediterranean guesthouse bungalows. Webster slows, walks, breathes hard heavy; some salt stings his eyes, sweat streams; and this is only the fourth day, Webster. Your shape returns slowly, doesn't it? Those seven semisedentary years cost you; and just at the wrong time; mid-thirties. Thigh muscle flutter and leg wobble? Runs again to keep from collapse. Webster wind-sprints to the guesthouse he and Laura share.

Glances in the bedroom in passing; Laura sleeps; sweat clothes in the laundry hamper, dons swimming trunks still damp from yesterday's use, shivers, bathrobe and towel over the arm. That annoying whirr again. Phone from the mansion.

"Hello."

"Heddley, sir." The very proper butler.

"Yes, Heddley."

"A gentleman to see you, sir."

"His name?"

"A Mr. John Barton, sir." Modest clearing of his throat.

"You want to add something, Heddley?"

"Yes, sir. I believe he is the sheriff of this county, sir."

"Oh."

"Yes, sir."

"Did he say what he wants?"

"No, sir. He merely asked to speak to you."

"All right. Bring him out to the pool. I'll be there in a few minutes."

"Yes, sir. Very good, sir."

Bare feet in the grass. Cool. Slight breeze sweat shiver. Swimming pool and terrace on the far side of the mansion. Thick man, solid. Middle age, thinning straw hair, light brows, slate-gray impassive eyes. Powder-blue uniform and Stetson, cartridge belt, but no gun. Not the pistol macho type, Webster. His hands thrust in pockets, cigarette dangling in a solid workmanlike face, dusty suede boots; looks real enough, Webster.

"Sheriff Barton?"

"Yes, sir. You're Mr. Daniels?" Proffered hand taken; strong grip, but no attempt to squeeze hard; no sense of his trying to awe you, Webster.

"Webster Daniels, yes. What can I do for you?"

Devil's Adversaries

"Well, sir, that's a kind of delicate thing. Maybe it might help if I could ask you a few questions. If you don't mind, of course. There's no obligation."

"I'll know better about that after I hear the questions." Smile when you say that, Webster.

The sheriff smiles too, easily, "That's sensible. You're a houseguest of the Sloans?"

"Yes. My friend, Laura Deveraux, was a college friend of Mrs. Sloan."

"Uh-huh. Any special reason for your visit? Or is it just, oh, a sort of spontaneous thing?"

"The latter."

"Any particular length of time you're planning on being around these parts?"

"No. Nothing particular, just as we enjoy it and seem to be enjoyed."

"Uh-huh. Well, sir, that brings us to the delicate part. Seeing you're a houseguest of an eminently respectable household, I kind of hate to bother you like this. The thing is, though, you're not, mmmm, unknown, Mr. Daniels. You have a reputation, what with this book of yours and your appearing on TV and so forth. If you'll excuse my saying so, it's not the kind of reputation that a law-enforcement officer likes to see in his jurisdiction."

"I can understand that, Sheriff. To a certain extent, I can even sympathize with your position, but at this late date, I don't see how I can change the situation."

"Yes, sir. The thing is, what's past is past as far as the law is concerned. The limitations thing has wiped the slate clean. I'd just feel real comfortable if I knew it was going to stay that way."

"As I say, I sympathize with your position, Sheriff. However, personal assurances from one with, as *you* say, my

The Devil and Webster Daniels

reputation hardly seem likely to satisfy you. So I suppose all we can do is await the events."

He rocks on his heels gently, removes his Stetson and fiddles with the brim, turns it slowly round in his large comfortable hands. Sighs. Webster walks to the edge of the pool and dives in, swims a length, pauses by the side in the shallow end as Barton approaches. He squints down at you, Webster, as if you're a cut of meat he doesn't think he wants to buy. Rocks gently on his heels.

"Was there something further, Sheriff?"

"I think so."

Webster waits. "What you said. Awaiting the events. There's where I have to disagree with you. I just can't afford to do that and still run a peaceable county. A fair percentage of good law enforcement is preventative. You have to anticipate. That's why I came out here as soon as I heard in Brewster that you were a houseguest of the Sloans'."

"The principle seems sound, Sheriff, but in this case, how and what do you anticipate?"

"Well, I had the impression from what I read of you, might be wrong, but I had the impression you are a kind of cocky fellow. Seeing what you did and managed to get away with, maybe you got a right, but it occurs to me that a fellow with your, uh, special ideas might think it was sort of humorous to pull off a few more stunts just after telling about the ones you did before. Seems like that might appeal to a man with your kind of imagination. And we've got quite a few wealthy people around here. Quite a few."

"I've got all the money I need and want, Sheriff."

"Yes, sir, I know you're a wealthy man, but if I read right, you didn't just do it for money. Pull your stunts. Seems like you like to make a point."

Webster smiles up at him. "You read right, Sheriff. I didn't do it just for the money."

Devil's Adversaries

He nods. "Uh-huh. That's what I thought and I said to myself, 'John Barton you better go have a talk with this fellow,' and that's what I'm doing, and I said to myself, 'John Barton you better keep an eye on that fellow,' and that's what I'm going to do." Sets his hat squarely on his head and looks you in the eye, Webster. "If my suspicions are unfounded, and I admit more often than not this kind of thing doesn't come to anything, if they're off the mark, why I apologize in advance. And my keeping an eye on you will be done so as not to embarrass you as long as you don't try to pull any stunts. But that's the way I see my duty and I'm a man who does his duty as he sees it." Pauses to give you a chance to reply, Webster.

"As I say, Sheriff, I understand and sympathize with your position. Someone keeping an eye on me won't bother me, one way or the other."

"That's right nice of you, Mr. Daniels." Touches the brim of his hat. "My respects to the Sloans and I sincerely hope I don't have cause to bother you again. Enjoy your stay in Putnam County, Mr. Daniels." Turns and walks away. Proud walk. Webster swims.

Moments of motion in water make you evolutionary-minded; glimpse of sky, tree, chrome table leg, red tile squares, water; what water dreams, ape acts, horde huddles brought you to this pool, Webster?

Glimpse water, red tile squares, webbed chrome chair, bush, sun, sky, fan of leaves, underside of newspaper on glass table top, red tile squares, water. Loss of self-consciousness. Being with the water, not it, not in it, with it. Rhythm. Not water and not Webster, just motion and glimpses and being with the water. Water, red tile squares, heaped bathrobe and towel, stone wall, cloud.

Until the breathing labors again and you pull up in the shallow end and climb from the pool and towel dry and put

The Devil and Webster Daniels

on the bathrobe. Then you are Webster again. Webster walks slowly across the manicured lawn toward the guesthouse thinking about the sheriff of Putnam County.

Bob Dylan; "Outlaw Blues."

The sheriff is thinking of you, Webster, as he talks to his chief deputy, Harry Reynolds, just outside the gate of the Sloan estate.

"You know what he looks like and you know the Sloan cars. If he comes out, you follow. Nice and discreet, but don't lose him."

"You mean he knows I'm going to be tailing him? He expects to be followed?"

"Yeah, that's right. So it doesn't matter that he sees you, just don't sit in his lap. I don't want the Sloans making any complaints about police harassment."

"But don't lose him."

"That's right, Harry. I wouldn't want to have to go and get a new chief deputy after all the work I got in training you for the job."

"Okay, Jack. You can trust me to do it right. That's what I get paid for."

"That's right. And if he's foolish enough to try one of his tricks, you get him, hold him, and get me fast."

"Sure, Jack."

"Okay, Phil will relieve you at nine tonight. If he's on the move, make sure you keep the office informed where you are."

"Right."

Barton takes it easy, relaxed, driving back to the office. Fall sun is sweet and your favorite season isn't it, Jack? Feels good to have it all under control, just like the easy way you slide

Devil's Adversaries

your Ford Interceptor into the turns and glide in and out of traffic on interstate 84; glance at the bluing Berkshires wooded distant slopes; only occasionally think that at eighty miles an hour, on this wide, high-dual highway carved through foothills and small rises, you are always just a couple inches bad judgment with the wheel away from the edge; control is merely an illusion that works as long as it works, but if you lose it, if you go over, you only have a span of seconds to let the reality coming up to greet you repair the error of your philosophy.

Funny fellow, this Daniels. Seems to have liked living on the edge. But why? A better view of the drop? What these writers call a heightened consciousness? Some times must have to seem silly to you, to dwell on the fall all take sooner or later; when you go down, you go down; why think about it? Now and then, though, even you think about it; almost a dozen years as sheriff and within sight of fifty and what do you have to show for it? Your own kind of integrity is the only answer you can come up with and it's not a very marketable commodity.

At the office, the mail is uninteresting and the routine is routine. Can't make yourself sit behind the desk and do the overdue paperwork, can you, Jack? Got to get out in the car and drive some more on a day like this. Maybe you ought to go over to see this Allenby; have a little talk with him, too; but he's a bit harder to pin down; you don't know yet what approach to take with him. So relax, Jack. Tool around your county. Make a few calls on the political people you need to touch base with. Next year is another election and it's tough to be an elected Democrat in upstate New York. Real tough.

Blood, Sweat and Tears; "Smiling Phases."

The Devil and Webster Daniels

Laura sits at the breakfast table with coffee and a cigarette. She yawns at him as he comes in, sits beside her.

"Morning, love. Finished all your exercise?"

"It just about finished me. I wonder if I'm getting too old for this kind of thing?"

"Got the blues?"

"A bit."

"Why?"

"Well, for one reason, I had a chat a few minutes ago with the local sheriff."

Her eyes widen; she is awake. "Do tell." Webster tells. Laura frowns; puzzled jade eyes; shrugs. "I don't quite see what there is to get upset about. We knew when you decided to publish *Diamonds* that we would encounter a little frost from local law someplaces."

"Yes, but I didn't think I'd be trying to pull another job. Maybe it *is* too dangerous."

Skeptic. "Come on, Webster. I don't believe that's you. You're not serious about being afraid. You're just focusing my attention on what a whiz you're about to put over."

Webster laughs. "Maybe I am at that."

Webster and Laura in casual clothes borrow one of Vera's cars; restored blueberry '46 Ford coupe; three-mile drive down route 22 into the village of Brewster. Sunny day. Pleasant drive. Fellow travelers.

"I hate to say anything, Webster, but hasn't that beige sedan been following us right along?"

"Yes."

"Sheriff Barton?"

"No."

"One of his deputies?"

"I expect so."

"So, he's a man of his word."

"Evidently."

Devil's Adversaries

"My God, Webster, I've never heard you so laconic before." Clothing stores. Webster outfitting. Black navy watch cap. Black turtle-neck jersey. Black denim pants. New sneakers. And everywhere that Laura and Webster went, the beige sedan was sure to follow.

The Kingston Trio; "Shoot the Deputy Down."

Dinner party at the main house; formal wear; guests on the terrace for champagne. Webster knows him at once. Large man, taller than Webster's six-two even, moves with a presence, almost a menace, without seeming to move at all. Blink your eye and he is standing next to you, looking down at you. Sleek black hair tight like a skull cap; anthracite eyes; a heavy face.

Smile, Webster; extend a hand. "You're Edward Allenby."

"Yes." His smile is only on his full lips, not in the eyes, and looks almost like a pout. "You're Webster Daniels." The hand is fleshy, but firm; strong grip; cold skin. Turns. "And this must be the lovely Laura." Grasps her hand in both of his, seems suddenly close to her, almost overwhelming, as if to ingest her. Webster twitches, startled; his hand moves halfway up and out toward them; to do what, Webster? Noticing, his smile now is in the eyes too and hard to meet and not pleasant. "Nerves, Mr. Daniels?" As if without moving, he is gone. Webster and Laura look at each other.

"I doubt if he's the devil, but I can see why Vera thinks so. He is one spooky dude. Did you see how I jumped?"

Laura nods. "Sexy too."

Lift your brows, Webster. "Really?"

"Oh, yes. Definitely."

"I wouldn't have thought he was your type, love."

25

The Devil and Webster Daniels

"Oh, he's not, but he definitely exudes an aroma of carnality." Smiles at you. "Jealous?"

"Of course not."

"Look at that, Webster." Turns his head; there are twenty or so guests, all couples save only Allenby; eight of the women are in a tight half circle in front of Allenby.

"Yeah. I'll be damned."

"There certainly is something about him. No wonder Vera is spooked by him."

"Yes. Some kind of sinister aura."

Heddley in the doorway; very tall and lean, very correct. "Dinner is served."

Seven courses of haute cuisine and you have to go easy, Webster; you're trying to take weight off; besides, gout is no longer a fashionable disease.

Afterward, on the terrace, sipping champagne in the chill of early evening, Allenby approaches again. Keep your nerve this time, Webster?

"I understand you're a chess player, Mr. Daniels."

"Yes and a romantic too. I often think that G. Gordon Liddy and I are the last two profound romantics in the modern world." That's better, Webster. Bring back the cool.

"Seems an odd combination. Chess and romanticism."

"Yes, it is. Happily, I find life more amusing with inherent contradictions."

"I quite agree. We should have a game."

Webster nods. "We will. That's why I came."

He smiles and bows ever so slightly. "Wonderful, Mr. Daniels. You seem to have recovered your nerve. I was afraid you were not going to be much of a competitor. I was afraid you were not going to live up to your advance publicity."

Webster nods again. "So few do."

"Precisely. Shall we see if Mrs. Sloan has a board?"

Webster shrugs. "Do you need one?" Much better.

Devil's Adversaries

Allenby bows and smiles again. "Not if you don't. White or black?"

"I prefer black."

"So do I."

Webster takes a coin from his pocket, tosses it in the air. "Call it."

"Tails." The coin rings on red tile, spins, falls flat. "Tails it is. Your move, Mr. Daniels."

"Pawn to king four."

"You are a student of Bobby Fischer?"

"Not really. It's one of the oldest openings and one of the best."

"I quite agree. Pawn to queen four."

"Pawn takes pawn."

Allenby's eyes widen slightly. "So you do not decline queen's gambit? Queen takes pawn."

"I don't like to decline a man's favorite game. Then he has no cause for complaint when he is beaten. Knight to king's bishop three."

Allenby smiles. "And if you are beaten, Mr. Daniels?"

"I never complain."

"Marvelous. Queen to king five. Check."

"Queen to king two."

"The experts don't agree with you on that move, Mr. Daniels."

"Yes, but playing blindfold chess, I find it useful to try some unorthodox moves. Helps you to discover if your opponent is really creative or plays by rote. And chess has far too many variables to confine yourself to the merely orthodox."

"Queen to queen four."

"Pawn to queen four."

"Bishop to king's knight five."

"Queen to queen's knight five. Check."

The Devil and Webster Daniels

"Marvelous." He laughs. "I fear I have played too whimsically with you, Mr. Daniels. I topple my king."

Your turn to bow, Webster. "You are too generous. We will play again other times."

"Certainly. It appears it will be quite amusing. Until then, Mr. Daniels." He walks away.

Webster sips champagne. Much better. Some of the old adrenalin flowing, some of the feel coming back.

Midnight. The other guests have gone. Webster, Laura, and Vera in the sitting room of the guest bungalow. Webster has told them of the blindfold chess game.

"What do you think, Webster?"

Webster sips scotch. "I don't know, Vera. There certainly is something about him. I had the feeling that he knew exactly what I was here for. That hardly seems reasonable, but I felt he knew and was, just as he said, amused by the prospect."

"See, I told you."

"You said he was the devil. I haven't seen any evidence of that, yet. I'll grant you he might be a warlock."

"When . . . when do you think you might . . ."

"Soon, Vera. A few more days and I'll be in reasonable enough shape. I have to get some equipment and scout out his place."

"Oh."

"What?"

"I forgot. He invited you and Laura and I to a late luncheon at his estate tomorrow. Around one-thirty."

"That's uncanny."

"Yes, it is, Laura."

Vera looks doubtful. "Should we go?"

"Why not?"

"I don't trust him."

"Not necessary. All we have to do is be cleverer than he is."

Devil's Adversaries

"I know, but—"

"Not to worry." Laura laughs. In the half light of a single lamp his crooked smile reminds you of the old Webster with the battered nose and scarred incredible face.

"I haven't heard you say that in years, love."

"No one we know has been worried in years."

Later, Webster and Laura walk. Drift slowly across the acres of lawn. November moon and a real chill in the air now.

"You're restless these days, Webster."

"Yes."

"Why?"

He sighs. "Something . . ."

"Doing it again? Being back into an . . . adventure?"

"It seemed clear to me before. What I was doing and why. I had to recreate myself and it had to be in opposition to" —he waves an arm in the general direction of the city—"all that."

"And now?"

"The doing it was okay, the process, but . . . what it became is . . . unsatisfactory. You're the only part of it that remains beautiful."

Then they are naked, standing, looking at one another. Her nipples are hard as jewels and their skin is cold. They lie down in moonlit grass and renew the perishable warmth of love.

Duke Ellington; "Sophisticated Lady."

After his morning workout, Webster drives to town in the blueberry coupe. Again, he is followed. He meets Bobbie Deams at the railroad station. They drive to a small roadhouse bar.

The Devil and Webster Daniels

In a back booth, Bobbie opens a compact black leather bag, not unlike a doctor's bag. An assortment of lock picks, cutting devices, electronic miniature amplifier with earplug, pencil flash, small lantern with a funnel lens.

"I think everything you wanted is there, Webster. It's all the best, too."

"Yes, it's all the right things, Bobbie. Thanks. How much did it run?"

"Forget it, boy. You made me. Made my life. It's the least I can do."

"Okay, Bobbie. Thanks again. Did you find out anything about Allenby?"

"Nothing much prior to his coming here. He showed up here about two years ago and bought his place, started moving in moneyed circles. Opened a sizable account at the Brewster Federal with a check on the Bank of Nova Scotia, Bahamas branch. You know how that is—they're tighter than the Swiss when it comes to passing out information. Sorry, but that's the crop."

"Don't be. I really didn't expect too much. He doesn't seem the sort of man to leave a background lying around for casual inspection."

"I could dig a little more."

"No. It's really not too important. Just idle curiosity. When are you going back to Amsterdam?"

"Another two or three weeks. I'm enjoying myself, but I'm not really suited to life in the states any more."

"I know what you mean." Webster raises his glass and Bobbie follows suit. "To crime."

"To crime."

Bob Dylan; "Subterranean Homesick Blues."

Devil's Adversaries

Allenby's house, set back from the road a quarter mile and shrouded by a small encircling forest of pines, is a large square one-story Spanish-style villa built around a central courtyard. As the coupe breaks through the pines and swings into a graveled parking, turning circle, a huge man rounds the far corner of the house; nearly seven feet and three hundred pounds stretch and bulge his casual clothes; straining against his left arm are three heavy snarling wolves on leashes. He stops thirty feet or so away and stands watching the coupe as the three emerge.

Vera waves and calls to him, "It's all right, LeSsave. Mr. Allenby is expecting us." He disappears back around the corner. They begin to walk toward a trio of arches that is repeated on each side of the house and which leads to the central courtyard.

"You neglected to mention that fellow and his pets, Vera."

"I know, Laura. I was afraid Webster wouldn't want to . . . uh, deal with them."

"What other cute surprises have I got coming?"

"None, Webster. I swear no more surprises."

"That you know of."

"Well, yes."

"Terrific."

Allenby appears in the center arch as if conjured to greet them. He is dressed in a three-quarter-length turtle-neck jacket and trousers of black fur.

A slight bow. "Welcome to my dwelling. I trust LeSsave did not alarm you?" Seems to be smiling at you, Webster.

"No, no. Charming. Must be a comfort to have around the house. And those cuddly little dogs. So cute."

"Better and better, Mr. Daniels. You do not disappoint me. It is so seldom one makes a new acquaintance who is truly amusing. But come, we shall have drinks before our luncheon."

The Devil and Webster Daniels

He leads the way across the courtyard; the tile squares are black except for a pattern of orange ones which describe a pentagram around the perimeter which encloses a five-pointed star and in the center of the star is what appears to be a chessboard, orange and red squares each two feet to a side; each orange tile of the pentagram and star has a large hole in its center as if for a post.

"Interesting design in the courtyard, Mr. Allenby."

"Thank you, Mr. Daniels. It is, of course, a design in more than the casual sense of that word."

"Blood rites?"

A look of longing pleasure fills his face; the full sensual mouth is languid with contemplation.

"Alas, only when necessary, Mr. Daniels. And that is so seldom."

"Too bad."

"Yes."

Entering the far arches, Allenby indicates a leftward direction and they pass through a heavy wood door into a large oval windowless room with walls of oriental-patterned carpeting in primary colors; the floor and ceiling are mirrors and the only furniture is four semireclining chairs and four small tables, all of soft translucent plastic; lying in them is a disturbing sensation, Webster; almost as if you were floating on air, and stiff drinks and the heat of the room don't help.

LeSsave appears with fresh drinks and individual plates of hors d'oeuvres. Deviled eggs and a chilled cup of deviled crab? You can hardly believe that, Webster; raise your brows at him. Allenby smiles and nods gently.

"My own recipes."

Webster laughs, hard, long, and Allenby joins him.

"I'm glad you appreciate my little joke, Mr. Daniels. One does so love to have one's sense of humor appreciated."

Steaming, spicy, hot curried lamb served with an elegantly

chilled Bordeaux; heightened sense of taste, Webster? A clearer vision and a sense of leisure? Strangely little conversation? A ring of profiteroll made with devil's food cake? More laughter. Thick, gritty Turkish coffee and a strange liqueur in tiny long-stemmed crystal goblets; clear liquid with a licorice taste.

"Absinthe?"

"Yes."

Now the heat is oppressive and the sense of heightened awareness approaches pleasure accompanied by pleasant sense of loss of will. A kind of freedom? Like four in levitation, the images in the ceiling reflect the images in the floor reflect the images in the ceiling; so many selves, Webster; so casual.

Allenby smiles and his words seem to come so slowly, yet so precisely, each one inflating in his head until it forces the mouth open and escapes gently; drift out as if you could see them; puffed and pompous portents.

"Of . . . course . . . the . . . food . . . was . . . drugged."

That is hysterical. Webster and Vera and Laura laugh. Giggles first. Then deep booming, rolling, rollicking merriment. And twisting, writhing, red-faced, breath-gasping, and wet-eyed crescendo. Slowly subsides. Torso aches and the head pops clear for a second and everything is as cold as the shivering sweat on your brow, Webster. Then drift up to a new level of calm contemplation content well-being.

"It is a . . . compound of . . . my . . . own . . . making. . . . I'm . . . glad . . . you . . . find . . . it . . . enjoyable."

The lights dim and then go out. A tiny beam focuses on the center of the ceiling. Expanding, it is a pale pink flower. A pale blue flower. A pale yellow flower. Spinning slowly. A white rose. Spins faster. A blood-red rose. Spins so fast it almost seems not to be spinning at all. A red circle around a white circle around a red circle around a white circle around

The Devil and Webster Daniels

a red circle. Expanding and contracting. High thin flute music.

"You . . . are . . . entering . . . a state . . . like . . . sleep. . . . You . . . see . . . you . . . feel . . . you . . . will . . . remember . . . but . . . you have . . . no . . . will. . . . You . . . can . . . not . . . move . . . except . . . by . . . my . . . command. You . . . will remain . . . here . . . a . . . long . . . time . . . while . . . LeSsave . . . prepares . . . you . . . and . . . it . . . will . . . seem . . . merely . . . an . . . instant."

His shadow floats around the room as he comes to each and kisses each on the mouth. Warm sweet breath and fur tickle. Distant sound of many doors closing. Tranquil silence save only soft breathing. LeSsave in the room. Disrobes them. Departs. Tranquil silence, soft breathing.

A double door opens to the courtyard and night sky. LeSsave looms large, lifts Webster lightly in his chair, transports him to the courtyard. Each tile hole holds a tall black candle making a star of fire within a pentagram of fire. In the center stands . . . Allenby? His face is red; his skin is red. He has a long sharp mustache and a small pointed goatee. Sharp ears seem prominent and two pale red bumps protrude from high in his hairline. The three wolves lie motionless at his feet.

LeSsave sets Webster in a tip of the star. Returns with Laura, sets her in an opposite tip. They do not mind the cold air, barely feel it. He murmurs to the wolves at his feet; one arises and pads silently to stand by Webster, another by Laura; LeSsave lays a fur robe at Allenby's feet. He carries Vera and lays her on the robe. Stripping hirsute muscular body, he takes Vera, coldly, rapidly. Sobs are torn from her. Hear the excited wolf breath, Webster?

Rerobed, he stands, arms folded across his chest, anthracite eyes burning. LeSsave extinguishes the candles; first the star; now the pentagram; brings their clothes and dumps them on the tile.

"You may go now."

He walks away followed by the wolves, followed by LeSsave; they disappear through the double doors; the doors shut.

It seems a long time before Webster and Laura can move. Wind blows through the courtyard. Vera's sobs are continual.

Dressed, they help her dress, lead her to the car; Laura holds her in her arms all the way back to the mansion. Heddley helps them get her to bed. A doctor comes, sedates her.

Laura and Webster in the bungalow. Shower separately and for a long time. The steam feels wonderful, Webster, but it can't get inside your head. They sit in the living room in bathrobes. Sober now. Smoke and find conversation hard. Laura shudders.

"She said, she told me, after the doctor left, just before she went to sleep, she said the horror was that for a few minutes she enjoyed it. Wanted him . . . wanted him to have the power over her . . . wanted to be, well, it's melodramatic, but wanted to be violated in some final, some absolute sense. That was the horror she said."

"Easy, love. There's no sense reliving it. What time is it?"

"Time?"

"Yes. What time is it?"

"I don't know. I left my watch in the other room."

Webster goes and looks, returns. "Ten-thirty. It seems as if it should be two or three in the morning."

"Does it matter?"

"No, I guess not. Don't mind me love. I'm disoriented."

"I know what you mean."

The Devil and Webster Daniels

Webster stands by her, absent-mindedly rumples her hair. Footsteps. They look at each other. The door swings noiselessly open; Allenby in the room. No mustache, no goatee, casual slacks and a nylon windbreaker; looks quite ordinary. Smokes a cigarette in a three-inch cheap black plastic holder.

"The, uh, little demonstration of my will, my power, of . . . who I am was for your benefit, Mr. Daniels."

"Yeah. I guess I forgot to thank you."

"You see, I'm rather a fan of yours. I read your book and I feel that your philosophy is somewhat like mine." Webster shaking his head. "You disagree, but you just haven't thought it out. You haven't logically extended. You were repulsed by the demonstration, but that is, in your own words, your conscience. Not mine. If you are willing to abdicate your conscience to no one, then you may not ask me to abdicate mine to you. I can live with, I rather enjoy, the implications of our philosophy. The question is, Can you?"

"I can live with the implications of my philosophy."

"Excellent. I hope you can still say that once you've thought it through. I believe you can; I believe you will. I believe it so strongly, I'm quite willing to put it to a stern test."

"A test?"

"Yes."

"What kind?"

He pulls a sheaf of papers from his jacket, walks over, extends them to Webster. Webster remains motionless, makes no move to take them. Allenby sets them on a table by the door.

"Those are affidavits, duly sworn, witnessed, and notarized of the occurrences at my dwelling today. You may present them to the local State's attorney's office if you choose. Depending upon the interpretation of the law they are

Devil's Adversaries

evidence of either four or five felonies punishable by what would amount to a life-imprisonment sentence."

"You must be joking."

"I am always jesting, but the situation is as I have described it. The papers are genuine."

"What makes you think I won't use them?"

A slight bow. "My estimation of you. You see, Mr. Daniels, the only truly worthy adversary is one who sees the world as you do. The only difference between us is of a degree. You value some things that I do not."

"You say."

"Yes, I do." Turns to go, pauses. "You mustn't worry about Vera. She's not important. She was only a device. You are the one who matters." The doorway is empty. Cold wind comes in.

Webster goes over, looks out, closes the door. Takes the papers to a chair and carefully reads through them.

"That's what they are. Just what he said." Lays them aside. "Sinister is too mild a word. He's almost got me believing he is the devil."

"I agree with everything, but the almost."

"Are you serious?"

"I guess not. I guess the drugs and the hypnotism made the candles, makeup, mumbo jumbo seem real."

"I wonder."

"What are you going to do, Webster?"

"With the papers?"

"Yes."

"I don't know, Laura. What do you think?"

"Vera's no saint, but she's not vicious; she's not evil. She's just rich and a little silly, but what he did . . ."

"That doesn't answer the question."

"No. I can't. He gave them to you."

"I know, but you're involved too."

Silence. Rain starts. They sit immobile as if painted. Rain.

Laura moves to him. Kneels and lays her head in his lap. They turn out the lights, go to bed, make love; at first it is not good, they startle themselves; later it is and she cries with relief; he wants to. Rain. Sleep.

Cold damp glum morning; Webster runs; Webster swims. The pool and the tile and sky again. Footsteps; boots and gray trouser legs; squeaking of a poolside chair. Webster hooks crossed forearms over the pool's edge, half hangs, half floats by the side, looks up at the seated sheriff. Barton semi-reclines, legs stretched out straight, ankles crossed; his Stetson is tilted forward and down. He looks at Webster.

"I would say, good morning, Mr. Daniels. Only I don't think it is and I don't feel like it."

"Forced amenities are worse than none at all."

"Yeah. That's you. That's just the kind of thing I'd expect you to say. You're probably right."

"Does the morning's lack of goodness have something to do with the reason for your visit, Sheriff?"

"Yeah. I didn't want to have to come up here again, but it looks to me, the way things are going, I probably didn't make myself clear the first time I came."

"I thought you were very lucid."

"Well if I was, I got to think, the way things are going, we got a problem."

"How are things going? As you see it?"

"I told you I'd keep an eye on you and I've had a couple of men doing it."

"I know."

"Well, sir, when they report to me that you've been in Brewster buying some things and you met this Deams fellow

Devil's Adversaries

and he went into the restaurant carrying a little black equipment bag and you came out with it and when I check on his recent movements with some people in the city and find out he's been buying some special tools of your profession and you and your young lady and Mrs. Sloan visit this strange Allenby duck and when you come back Mrs. Sloan is mighty upset about something and a doctor has to come in and sedate her so she can rest—well, sir, after hearing all that, I got to figure either I didn't make myself too clear or we got a problem."

"What do you envision as the nature of the problem we have, Sheriff?"

"I think you think I'm just too dumb to bother with. I say to myself, John, he thinks you're just a dumb old country boy that he don't have to worry about. I am an old country boy, but not that dumb, Mr. Daniels. Maybe you don't know I'm a Democrat."

"I was not aware of your political affiliation, no."

"Maybe you have some idea how difficult it is to be a four-term elected official as a Democrat in this county or anywhere upstate."

"I can imagine."

"Then maybe you can imagine why I keep getting elected sheriff of this county. I keep getting elected because I keep on top of things, Mr. Daniels. People around here like things nice and quiet, no fuss, no problems. We've got the lowest crime rate per capita of any county in New York State. You got to know I know this Allenby's a strange one. I find out things about everybody that moves into my county and I know this bird is running some kind of funny game with a lot of well-to-do women around here. I'm not dumb, Mr. Daniels." There are seams in his face this morning, Webster. Tired lines. And angry.

"It never crossed my mind that you were."

The Devil and Webster Daniels

"All right, say it didn't. Let me put it to you nice and direct. Something is happening that involves Allenby and Mrs. Sloan and some other women around here. Something either illegal or . . . say, threatening to the peace."

"Is that a question?"

"Yes."

"Yes, something is happening. Metaphorically, there is a conflagration in your county. And it is a threat to tranquillity."

"And you're proposing to take a hand in it?"

"Yes."

"Heaping coals on it?"

"Hopefully, more in the nature of a fireman. In that sense our interests run parallel, Sheriff."

"What about the law?"

"It has already been broken by this fire, but it is in the nature of a violation that is very difficult to secure complaints from the victims. Legal complaints." He sighs, Webster, looks away from you. Looks up into the gray chill sky.

"Extortion?"

"I've already said more than is discreet, Sheriff. I would think, though, that a perceptive man like yourself would not always need corroboration to accept the fruits of his reasoning as accurate."

"These parallel interests, you're proposing that I give you a free hand to, uh, play fireman?"

"I don't see how you can avoid it if you expect to stop the fire without burning down your, uh, community. Let me put it this way: If I had proof of the illegal acts that I know have taken place, would you or the district attorney's office want them?"

"Why not?"

"Because to publicly try the felon would involve the destruction of the victims. The fire would be out, but the house would be ashes."

"Yeah." He stands up and walks away from you, Webster, paces at the far end of the pool.

Webster gets out of the pool, towels dry, puts on a bathrobe. When the sheriff is standing next to you, Webster, you're an inch or two taller, even in bare feet.

"If things are the way you say, it seems as if you've got me boxed in, Mr. Daniels."

"Call me Webster. Not me, Sheriff. Circumstantial combustion. You are boxed in because peace in your county is more important to you than the letter of the law and the situation is one where the law has little leverage."

"Suppose I agree that our interests are parallel?"

"Yes."

"Just how far into extralegal country do you think you'd have to go? There are some things I can't wink at. Not even for the sake of peace in the county. Some lines I couldn't cross and still live with myself."

"I'm not a violent man."

"No, I suppose not."

"Other than that, I suppose you'd have to rely on your assessment of me. I couldn't tell you what I'm going to do because I don't know yet. And I really don't think you want to know anyway."

"Yeah, that's one of the lines . . . Webster. I guess you better call me Jack."

"Thank you, Jack."

"You might let me know when you think you're ready to take a hand. I'd like to be ready to step in if . . . you can't put out the fire yourself—if it looks like it's going to spread."

"I can do that, Jack."

"Will you?"

"Sure." He turns as if to go, hesitates, turns back and looks at you, Webster. Extends a hand.

The Devil and Webster Daniels

"I guess I better shake your hand, Webster." They shake hands. "I hope I don't regret this."

"I hope neither of us regrets it, Jack."

"Yeah. I'll pull my men off. Let me know."

"Yes."

He walks away. In a minute the sound of a car engine comes. Webster watches the white car with the cherries on top down the drive and away, goes back to the bungalow for breakfast.

Simon and Garfunkel; "Keep the Customer Satisfied."

Webster has breakfast on the table when Laura comes out of the bedroom. He is kneeling by the fireplace, putting some papers on a small fire.

"What are you doing?"

"Burning Allenby's evidence."

"Oh." She sits and sips orange juice. "Then you decided."

"Not me. Circumstances. What we didn't think about when we were discussing it last night was what it would do to Vera and some of the other women involved if Allenby was prosecuted."

"Yes. That's right. So you thought of it."

"It came to me in my discussion with Jack Barton."

"Jack? Barton?"

"Yes, the sheriff and I are first-naming each other now. We are colleagues more or less."

"Do tell." Webster tells her. "What *are* you going to do?"

"Get the evidence. That's first. After that's done we can think about a proper . . . mmmm, resolution."

"Just like that, get the evidence he uses for blackmail, just like that?"

"Sure, why not?"

Laura shakes her head. "We underestimated him when we so blithely accepted his luncheon invitation."

"I know. I still believe he can be beaten."

"Maybe."

After breakfast, Laura goes up to the house to see how Vera is; Webster goes to the garage, then the kitchen. In the afternoon, it begins to snow. It snows steadily into the evening and by eleven o'clock several inches lie on the ground and the wind is making large drifts.

Webster in basic black; with the watch cap pulled down to just above the eyes, looks a bit like the old Webster. Feels a bit like the old Webster; nervous stomach, dry mouth, shaky hands; rookie jitters again; *déjà vu*.

Webster on the phone. "Sheriff Barton? Webster Daniels."

"Tonight?"

"Yes."

"You don't waste a hell of a lot of time. Bad weather for it."

"I'll manage. I need your help, though."

"How's that?"

"Do you have any, uh, oh unsolved crimes right now. Like a robbery or some reasonably serious felony?"

"Well, let's see. There was a restaurant holdup a couple weeks back."

"Could you pick up Allenby and his man LeSsave for questioning and hold them about four hours, then turn them loose?"

"I could. That's a kind of touchy thing, though. The ACLU is kind of active around here. Could make me look pretty bad."

"I assure you, Allenby won't look to the ACLU or the public for any redress of grievances."

"You assure me. And I take it."

The Devil and Webster Daniels

"Jack, it seems to me, you either rely on my judgment or you don't."

"Uh-huh. You play any poker, Webster?"

"Yes."

"Well, then you'd know what I mean when I say I feel like a man betting into a possible immortal."

"Five-card stud is a rough game."

"Especially if you play pot limit, which is what it seems to me we're doing here. Okay, I'll leave now."

Webster on the road in an International Scout; four-wheel drive on slick surfaces; an illusion of safety. Parks off the road, a couple hundred yards from the entrance to Allenby's estate. Waits.

At midnight, the sheriff's car pulls into the entrance, lights flashing; fifteen minutes later it comes back out.

Webster waits five minutes, goes on in. He approaches the side of the house and low, dark forms flicker in his headlights. As he stops, the vehicle is surrounded by wolves. They leap at the sides of the sedentary Scout, shake the windows, doors. Webster unwraps a brown paper package; three large steaks; rolls his window down an opening of two inches, pushes the steaks one by one through the opening to the snarling waiting jaws. The three fight over the first steak; two fight over the second; then each has his own.

"Eat hearty." Webster waits. Devouring the sixteen-ounce steaks is a short process; they circle the Scout, bellies full, tongues lolling, emitting occasional low growls. After a while, they stand and stare; then one sits down, rests his head in the snow; the other two fight encroaching sleep, succumb slowly. Webster waits. The sedative should make them sleep for six hours. At fifteen to one, he emerges. Drags them to the side of the house; leashes them with short lengths of chain to a pillar of one of the archways. Returns to the Scout; brings his black bag with him.

Devil's Adversaries

Circling the house looking for easy access, he finds a door to the kitchen has a small pane of glass; nothing fancy needed here; smash it out, reach in, and slip the bolt; inside. Play the flashlight about. The kitchen is large, well equipped; stone floor, tile walls. A door to the right. A mirrored, windowless hallway. Large wood door. A mirrored, windowless bedroom with modest appointments save an oversized bed at least nine feet long. LeSsave's room?

Another door. A narrow glass passageway with the grounds through arches on your right, the courtyard through arches on the left. Wooden door; mirrored, windowless bedroom much like the other, but the bed is standard double size; guest room? Door, hall, turns left, door; giant, mirrored, windowless bedroom with white fur carpet, a bed at least nine by twelve set on the floor Japanese style and covered by a black fur spread and half a dozen oversized white fur pillows; half of one wall a large fireplace and beside it sliding glass doors into a large bathroom—orange, black, red tile, sunken six-foot tub, large shower, dressing tables, cabinets; another wall is flush doors of closets with racks of clothing, including several dozen fur robes, half a dozen black and the rest white; no doubt about it, Webster. Allenby's room. Scan the walls. Nothing. Inside the closets nothing. The fireplace. Nothing. Or . . . funny little metal figures at the front corners of the hearth. Metal sculptures of devil figures with their feet sunk in concrete. Pull at one. Is there a little play, a little give, Webster? Shine the flash around. Is that a circular seam? Twist the statue. Clockwise, no give. Counterclockwise? Turns all the way around and lifts and beneath—the door of a barrel safe. Try the other one. Twins. And the locks are simple; pieces of cake—devil's food? I was afraid you were going to think that, Webster. Sorry about that. Open one; cans of film.

Open the other; cans of film. Take them out; open a can;

The Devil and Webster Daniels

sixteen-millimeter sound on film. Jesus. Shine the flashlight behind a few frames. Er, hmm, yes.

Open each can; eleven films, and all prints. That's all very well, Webster, but where are the negatives? Oh, well, it's a start. Drawstring burlap sack from the bag, film in the sack. Heavy load. And it's almost two. Better move it.

Door, glass passageway between arches, door; another bedroom; guest room. Door, hall, turns left, door; fifth bedroom. Door, glass passageway, door; library, heavy furniture, lamps, tables, small fireplace; quick scan of titles in the walls of bookshelves; each wall devoted to one subject—philosophy, theology, the sciences, the occult. A very interesting man, Mr. Allenby.

Door, hall looks familiar, door; the luncheon room with the clear plastic furniture—yecchht. Door, hall, door; kitchen. That's it then. Time—two twenty-seven. But they couldn't be jobbing these films out to an optical house; they'd have to do the work themselves. A basement? Well, try that door over there. Steps down. Furnace room, narrow passageway, large door, switch on the light. Jesus.

Twenty-five-by-twenty-five superfilm lab; developers, viewers, splicers, printers, cabinets with reels of raw film stock, chemicals, four sixteen-millimeter sound-on-film cameras; the works. But no negatives. Damn. Well, now what? Trash it? Seems a shame; several hundred thousand dollars worth of equipment. Oh, well. Trash it, Webster.

A large cement crock of . . . what are those symbols, can you remember your chemistry from NU . . . carbolic acid? Lift the lid carefully. Some kind of acid. All the film stock goes in, bubbles, vanishes. Put the cameras in; it may not dissolve them entirely, but they won't be worth a damn. Take a tripod mount and begin smashing things. Carefully at first. And not enough force. Enthusiasm builds. Shattering glass, battered metal, cabinets overturned and stomped. Kind of

Devil's Adversaries

fun, isn't it, Webster? And breath coming faster, shallower, whirling and battering, kicking, beating on the concrete floor and dizzy, excited and pause to survey your handiwork. Tortured, twisted, broken objects everywhere. Nothing stands. Except you, Webster.

Breath comes back and you can feel the face flush dying away. Drop the bent and useless tripod. Three-forty. Cutting it thin, Webster.

In the kitchen, take a small plastic chess piece from the bag; black bishop on an elastic thread; loop it on the doorknob. Exit, Webster.

The pets . . . pets? Oh well, pets are still sleeping. Webster throws the bag and sack in the back seat of the Scout, heads out the driveway. Exit, Webster.

And on the road, half a mile from the entrance, you pass a taxi taking them home. Honk vigorously and wave; they don't know who you are, but they'll soon figure it out. Exit, Webster, laughing. Laughing.

The Rolling Stones; "Midnight Rambler."

CHAPTER IV

The Devil's Due

Scout in the garage; Webster and goodies in the bungalow; Laura in his arms.
"You made it."
"Piece of cake."
"You say."
"But no negatives. Just these prints."
Webster tells her about it. When he describes the trashing, she frowns but, when he mentions passing the taxi, she laughs aloud.
"Webster, you *are* incorrigible."
"Sure, that's why you love me."
"We'll just let that pass. What about the negatives? What do we do about them?"

The Devil and Webster Daniels

"That's a good question."

"That's not an answer."

"No."

"Why did you bring the prints with you? Why didn't you put them in the acid with the raw film stock?"

"I guess I just didn't think about them while I was trashing the place. Afterwards, I had to get going. I cut it pretty thin."

"Yes, I'd say so. A margin of a minute or so."

Webster chucks the bag and sack into a cabinet under the sink. They go to bed; the love-making is a little stiff, uneasy some way; Laura seems some distant, thoughtful.

Webster is having bad dreams. Vanished dreams. Everything is gone. He is alone. Naked. As before.

The light snaps on in their bedroom. Laura and Webster start, shake themselves partially conscious, look. LeSsave is standing in the doorway. He sees they are awakening, motions to them.

"Come in here." Turns and walks to the living room. Allenby is sitting in an easy chair. He and LeSsave still have their overcoats on and gloves. The mantel clock reads six thirty-four; it is still dark outside.

"You have gravely disappointed me, Mr. Daniels."

"So sorry, old man, but let's discuss it at some other time. At a civilized hour." Allenby nods at LeSsave; Webster does not see the hand coming for the slap that sends him sprawling on the floor.

"You are hardly in a position to speak of civilized conduct. Perhaps, you now realize you are not in a position to be flippant either."

Webster's head is ringing. He stands up. "Reminds me of the old Jack Benny line to Fred Allen—'You wouldn't talk to me that way if my writers were here.'" Allenby nods and LeSsave hits Webster in the breastbone; fist feels like a truck and collapses him on his knees. Can't breathe and wonder if your heart stopped, Webster?

"Presently, your romantic posture will grow tiresome even to you, Mr. Daniels."

It's a long way up from the floor and even standing, a little hunched over and still fighting for breath, LeSsave is still above even a very tall man like you, Webster. His blond hair is thin and cut close to the skull. He stands completely relaxed, arms at his side. His face is impassive and his eyes take you in with complete indifference.

"You shouldn't have destroyed my laboratory, Mr. Daniels. That was petty and mean."

Webster sighs and shrugs. "You know how it is when you're slumming." LeSsave does not even wait for a nod; Webster is surprised by his speed again; quick combination, left to the stomach, right cross to the mouth. Back on the floor again. Laura has seized a poker from beside the fireplace and, two-handed grip, swings it down on LeSsave's forehead. A split appears and red fills it, but it only rocks him and he stares at Laura. She is stunned that he did not fall.

"Put the poker down, Miss Deveraux, or I shall have to let LeSsave hurt you."

"Better do it, love. He could break our necks with his hands." The poker clatters on the hearth. Webster is sitting. Blood runs from his mouth.

"I don't mind your destroying my films, though it is a bother to make new prints, but I expected some such move in our little competition. I don't even mind your using the sheriff in that manner. I can see a certain wit, a certain irony in that, but that crude, ugly mess. That offends me, Mr. Daniels. That offends me."

"Well, you know what they say, beauty is in the eye of the beholder. I know; I know. Now you nod at LeSsave and he hits me."

The Devil and Webster Daniels

"Just so." Allenby nods. LeSsave pulls Webster up with his left hand and holds the front of his pajamas; smashes him in the face three times with his right hand; Webster blacks out.

When the water brings you semiconscious, you wish it hadn't, don't you, Webster? Soaked, shivering, head throbbing, mouth full of blood and fragments of teeth, lumpy raw face, and you just know your nose is broken. Allenby is leaning over you.

"I must say your bravado is fairly impressive even if rather trite, rather outdated. Ordinarily, I don't allow myself to use this kind of crude force, but you did anger me. Truly, you did."

"Listen, Allenby, it's getting hard for me to think up any more lines. So if it's all the same to you, just have LeSsave finish up the hitting this morning and I'll mail you the wisecracks in a day or two."

LeSsave moves forward, but Allenby waves him back. Smiles a really nasty smile at you, Webster.

"More subtlety from now on. Or I fear this game won't be amusing any more."

Webster tries to sigh; can't with all the blood; lies flat on his back. "I wouldn't want to bore you. Did you ever think of taking up a hobby? Stamps, perhaps."

Allenby stands. "You probably ought to call a doctor, Miss Deveraux. Come, LeSsave." They are gone.

Laura is phoning the mansion, asking Heddley to send for the doctor. Webster is still on his back, staring at the ceiling.

"Whew. I thought they'd never go. I just hate people who try to keep a party going after all the fun has gone out of it."

"Don't try to talk, Webster. You don't have to be witty with me. I've always believed you are funny and brave."

Laura helps him to stretch out on the couch; gets an ice pack and washcloths for his face; holds his hand. When the

The Devil's Due

doctor comes, he wants Webster to go to the hospital, but he won't. The doctor patches what he can, leaves pain and sleeping pills. It is getting light outside as Webster goes to sleep again. Laura sits and watches over him.

What does Laura dream? Did Laura ever have any dreams at all? Poor little rich girl, free all her life. There doesn't seem much to ache for; when you're rich, intelligent, beautiful, anything is possible; all you have to do is reach out and make it happen.

So how did you wind up with a stylish thirty-nine-year-old thief who prizes wit and adventure? But who is Laura? Webster Daniels' lover and confederate? That just says who you go around with and do things with. Who is Laura?

A feeling so vague, images so ill-defined, thoughts so formless they almost aren't thoughts at all; tenuous almost to nullity.

And when you wake up in early afternoon, Webster, she is smiling down at you.

"Hi, love."

"Hi, yourself. You don't look so hot."

"People have said that to me before."

"Not recently."

And movement is pain in the ribs; the face feels raw; the head aches dully, rhythmically. Webster wonders if boxers go around all the time with a dull thudding inside the skull.

And look at you in the mirror, Webster. The nose, the plastic surgeon worked so hard to build up, is flat and spread again. The puffy rainbow tissue shows all the old scars you tried to tan over and the beginnings of some new ones. Your smile . . . smile? . . . better say grimace, shows gaps in the

The Devil and Webster Daniels

teeth again. The hair graft still keeps you from being bald again, but if it wasn't for that it would be back to square one; ugly Webster; mirror gargoyle.

The mustache needs trimming, but shaving is impossible. Take a shower. Get dressed. Sip the coffee Laura made for you.

"Well, love, how do you like it? Looks like LeSsave gave me back my old face."

Laura laughs. "I always loved it, Webster."

"Yes, I suppose I ought to be content. It's the real me. And I just don't see going through all that repair work again."

"No. You might do something about the teeth."

"Yes."

"Webster."

"Uh-oh. Don't think I care for that tone."

"I've been thinking."

"Anything I can help with?"

"I think, after this is over, I might want to go away for a while."

"Sure. We're going back to London."

"No. I mean by myself."

"Oh." That's like swallowing lead ingots; think of something witty, Webster. Can't, can you? "Well, you know all the standard questions."

"Yes, but the answer to all of them is no. It's not you or someone else. It's me."

He nods. "Permanent good-by, semipermanent, a vacation, what? Or don't you know yet?"

She smiles and touches one of his hands. "More like a vacation, I guess. I want to think about me. I want to think if I could be somebody, do something."

"Okay. You have to do what you have to do. You know me, Laura. I won't ever try to keep you from what you think you

The Devil's Due

want or need, but I do love you. I think we're good together. Don't make it any longer than you have to."

"I won't. I love you, Webster. I don't think I could ever just not see you, be with you again. I just need to think."

Webster nods, grins. "I know what you mean about that. The kind of life we've been leading atrophies the brain, the body, everything."

"That's why you feel so alive. Being back in an adventure. Doing your shtick."

"Funny, you don't look Jewish."

A knock on the door; they exchange glances.

"It can't be Allenby; he never knocks." Webster walks over and opens it; admits the sheriff; tattered old red mackinaw is his only clothing concession to the weather. "Come in and sit down, Jack. Oh, I don't believe you've met Laura. Sheriff John Barton, Ms. Laura Deveraux."

They shake hands, exchange pleasantries; the sheriff sits and accepts a cup of coffee. Eyes Webster's face.

"I hope you don't mind a personal remark, but your face looks like a pan of stew the dog stepped in."

"Ran into a door."

"Uh-huh."

"A very large door."

"About seven feet tall, three hundred pounds?"

"A very large door."

"You didn't, uh, finish your business fast enough?"

"No. I did. The door came to see me."

"You, uh, conclude your business? Successfully?"

"Partially. But copies of things are never as good as the originals."

The sheriff frowns. Sips coffee. "That's too bad. I was sort of hoping this could be wrapped up pretty quick."

"So was I." Webster is gently fingering his face; tests to see how sore the bruises and cuts and swelling are; very sore.

"What now?"

"Well, our friends will be buying some new equipment soon."

"Equipment?"

"For processing."

"I'll be damned. Right there in the house."

"It's not the sort of material you can send out to the corner druggist."

"No. I suppose not."

"And his equipment had an accident. A little like the door that came to see me. So if you could put some close surveillance on our friends . . . Let me know when new equipment begins arriving and, most important, if visits are made to some secure place."

"How's that?"

"A bank safety deposit vault, a club locker, something of that sort. The originals will be fairly bulky, not something you could really put in a briefcase."

"I see. But if this is the way it's going to go, why did the equipment have the accident? Tends to slow the process down."

"The accident was an irrational impulse. Not very well thought out."

Sheriff Barton smiles, seems to relax. "Nice to know you're just like the rest of us, Webster. Yeah, I believe I can make the arrangements you suggest. How about a little security for yourself and Ms. Deveraux? Just so the door doesn't come to visit any more."

"I don't think so, Jack. Not my style."

Barton nods. "I guess not. Suit yourself. Nice meeting you, ma'am." And he is gone.

Simon and Garfunkel; "Song for the Asking."

CHAPTER V

Beat the Devil

Webster in motion for days. Vera's dentist pulls the stubs of the broken teeth, three uppers, two lowers, all front. Makes two bridges.

Meets Bobbie Deams in Manhattan; needs some more tools. Sees Dave Reilly; asks him to get background on Allenby. Thinking vaguely of a potential denouement, asks Lina about film equipment and editors. And Laura goes along.

No word from Sheriff Barton for two weeks. Then a phone call.

"Webster? Jack Barton." Early December. The snow is off the ground, but days are hard frost, early dusk.

The Devil and Webster Daniels

"Getting some movement, Jack?"

"Some. A film-equipment-company van made a delivery to our friends this morning."

"Any idea of what?"

"Yeah, my deputy followed them for a while, then pulled them over. Routine search, he said. Told them we've been having some drug traffic in the county. Searched the van and made them show him copies of their bills of lading."

"Clever lad."

"Yeah, probably wants my job. One more term and he can have it. Anyway, he says some cameras, four I think, an editor and splicer, projector, raw film stock, developer chemicals, a developer, lot of other stuff. Odds and ends."

"I want to know when he gets those negatives."

"Yeah, I'll keep on them. You say hello to that nice lady of yours. That's about as good-looking a woman as I ever hope to see."

"I'll tell her that, Jack."

"You do that. And, Webster?"

"Yes."

"You're all right, you know."

"Coming from a man in your position, Sheriff, that's almost immoral, but I appreciate it."

Tom's Middlebranch Restaurant just outside Brewster; mid-December; snow again. Laura, Webster, Dave, and Lina in the L-shaped lounge; second drinks; chatting.

"We'll finish shooting in a couple of weeks. Dave is doing wonderfully. He's becoming a really fine actor."

"Yeah, I'm this terrific old neighborhood doctor that everybody loves who gets knifed by a speed-freak punk which gives honorable motivation for the cops to gun down six or seven citizens."

"All right, Dave, so it's not a great movie. It still doesn't change the fact that you're doing a great job."

Beat the Devil

"Thanks, honey, but just once I'd like a part in a decent film, where I don't get killed. You know, since I quit the insurance-investigator job and got together with Lina, I've made eleven pictures. And I haven't made it to the end of one yet. I have been killed in ten and died of a coronary in the other."

"You're working, Dave. That's more than most actors can say these days."

"Sure, but that's because you got me the parts."

"The first four, yes. I haven't influenced your career at all for years."

"Okay, okay. But, Lina darling, you must permit me not to take myself seriously. When you start a new career, a new life, in your fifties, in a field where you have no training, experience, or knowledge and you make a mild success, you've just got to know it's a fluke."

"Do something with him, Webster. He's hopeless."

"It seems to me he's striking just about the right pose. Hard working, interested in his craft, but with appropriate humility, self-knowledge, and balance. Perspective."

"That's a big help, Webster."

They move to the dining room. High ceiling, wide, very long rectangle. The glass wall at one end looks out at Lake Mahopac nestled in a trio of mountains covered with pine and birch. Cold blue light just before dusk. Steak, seafood, and veal dishes dominate the menu. Everyone has another drink and a shrimp cocktail.

Lina passes Webster a note sheet with four names and phone numbers on it. "Here's a list of editors that might be free in the next couple weeks to do a job for you, Webster. There are some others I didn't put down, but this four I know will do a good job."

"What will it cost?"

"I think any of them could do the job for five thousand."

The Devil and Webster Daniels

"Sounds okay."

"The background information I was able to get isn't very complete, Webster." Dave frowns. "Officially, at least, this Allenby is something of a cipher. I called in a lot of IOUs from old friends and didn't get much." He sips his drink. His face is concentrated and thoughtful and Webster almost smiles; he's still an investigator at heart, Webster. And any professional hates to come up empty. "My sources could find no background on him prior to nine months ago when he moved into Putnam County. He opened a substantial account at the Brewster National—"

"How substantial?"

"Seven figures, and not a minimum seven figures either. At least four or five million."

"Then why the hell should he get involved in a blackmail scheme that, at least by the standards of his wealth, is piddley ass?"

Dave shakes his head. "I pass. I've thought about it and I can't see it. Unless that was just a lead in."

"Lead in?"

"To get the women involved, sucked in for something more he has in mind."

"But what?"

"I don't know, Webster. I've thought about that too and I just don't know. Anyway, the account was opened with a letter of credit from the Bank of Nova Scotia, Bahamas branch. There are two things about that. First, because he used a letter of credit rather than a check, we can assume that the amount he deposited here is not all of his money. One of my sources said that the amount he has had transferred is not the top figure on the credit letter. He believes it was only about a third, so you have to figure this guy for having, at least, ten or twelve million dollars."

"And the other thing?"

Beat the Devil

"The Bank of Nova Scotia is a stone wall. They're more closemouthed than the Swiss."

"*That's* closemouthed."

"Yes. He entered the country at Miami on a Haitian passport, but he's not a citizen of Haiti."

"That's not reasonable."

"I know it's not, but I had a friend at the State Department check it out for me. The Haitian Government confirms that he has a valid passport, but is not a citizen and that's all they'll say. My friend told me that he has an indefinite visitor's visa which the department almost never issues, but he couldn't find out why. In fact, he sounded a little worried when he came back to me. Wanted to know why I wanted the information. I think he got into some trouble for poking around in Allenby's file, but he either didn't know why or wasn't saying."

"Well, what country is he a citizen of?"

"I don't know. I have several friends at Interpol and they have no records on him. I've tried sources I know in fifty countries and they all come up empty. I could pile up negatives all night long, but the simplest way to put it is that outside of having a Haitian passport, an indefinite visitor's visa in the states, and a lot of money, the guy just doesn't exist. In official terms anyhow."

"I don't know why, but it doesn't surprise me. Maybe he's got me spooked."

"Well, I'm damn sorry, Webster. I like to do better than this."

"You can't get what isn't there, Dave. Thanks for the effort." Dinner comes; on such a cold night everyone felt like having a nice steak; the dark is purple in places and you feel the mountains even when you can't see them.

The Devil and Webster Daniels

On weekends, when Caulder comes up from the city, there is some strain; he does not understand why Webster and Laura are staying around so long; he and Vera don't quite argue about it, don't discuss it directly, but he makes everyone uncomfortable. Webster wonders if they shouldn't rent a place of their own, but Vera likes having them there, says she needs Laura to talk to—it makes her feel safer. And Laura spends several hours a day with her; Webster only sees her at dinner in the mansion.

No reports from the sheriff. Webster goes for long walks in the snow. Likes the crisp air, mild exercise. Wonders what Allenby is doing. Then finds out.

The week before Christmas. Midafternoon, coming back from one more walk, sees the sheriff's unmarked car sitting in front of the bungalow. Inside, Laura and Barton are sipping hot chocolate, waiting for him. He gets a mug, sits.

"Something new, Sheriff?"

"Yes. You may not have to call me that much longer. The district attorney's office is investigating charges made against me by a Mrs. Shirly Harris of Fairfield County, Connecticut —you know, our neighbor just across the border."

"What charges?"

"Extortion, six counts. It seems I've been blackmailing Mrs. Harris for six months. A thousand dollars a month."

"What is supposed to have been your lever?"

"That's the clever part. She's been having an affair with one of my deputies, Harry Reynolds, for about a year. Claims I put the screws on when I found out about it."

"And?"

"I did find out about it nearly six months ago and went to see her. Harry's a pretty good man, got a nice wife and family, and I hated to see them get messed up. This woman, nice-looking young woman, wasn't interested in anything I, uh, had to say. Didn't give a damn about Harry's family.

Truthfully, I don't think she gave a damn about Harry either."

"Why?"

Barton reddened. "Well, sir, I hadn't been there very long when she, er, kind of pretended to take a liking to me. Made a bit of what you might call a pass. Got right nasty when I just kept trying to talk about why she should let Harry alone. After a while she just started singing and wouldn't listen to anything I said, so I left."

"Singing?"

"Yeah, that song, 'I'm Just Wild About Harry'; she just started singing it and didn't listen to anything I said."

Webster wonders. "Extortion. Certainly makes you wonder about our friend."

Barton nods. "She happens to be a friend of his. She visits him; he visits her."

"What about proof? Doesn't there have to be some kind of proof?"

Barton sighs. "Yes and that's the real nasty part. I've always thought a lot of Harry, but I guess he must want my job real bad. He gave the DA fifty-three one-hundred-dollar bills that he says he found in my desk when he was looking for an arrest form. The DA's office checked back and traced the money to Mrs. Harris's bank. She took out about twelve hundred a month cash the last six months and all in hundred-dollar bills."

"Money she was paying Allenby."

"That's what occurred to me. The thing I can't figure is Harry getting mixed up with Allenby. Or this whole thing."

"Maybe it's just him and the woman as far as he knows. Maybe she spurred his ambition."

"It's possible."

"What's going to happen?"

"The DA told me this morning about the investigation.

Courtesy, he called it. There's been a leak and it's going to hit the papers tomorrow. It doesn't help that he's a Republican either. He said he would decide next week whether or not to impanel a special grand jury and seek an indictment, but that's hoo-hah. He's already made up his mind; he's just trying to look judicious and fair."

"You'll pardon me saying it, Jack, but it looks like a flank attack. Allenby getting at me through you."

"I don't mind your saying it. It's what I think too. With me in trouble, you'll have a lot harder time moving freely around here. I can't protect you, with Harry and the DA looking for things to hang me with."

"I guess we'll just have to get you out of trouble, Jack."

"Sounds nice, but how do you figure to do it?"

"Oh, I think there's a way."

Webster and Laura visit Vera; drinks in the library; Webster explains the situation to Vera.

Vera listening pensively, sits in an easy chair, sips scotch and water; she drinks a bit more lately. Her long red hair looks well-cared-for today and she wears a smart pants suit. She is recovering a bit from the shock. And gearing up; her children come home from boarding school tomorrow.

"Yes, Shirly always was his special favorite. She didn't always go to the, uh, coven meetings, but when she was there, he was never with anyone else." She blushes. "Funny how silly it all seems when you're sitting here, comfortable, relaxed, in daylight or what passes for it at this time of year. Then I remember what it felt like when I was there. It was as if you had entered another level of reality . . . and left"— she gestures with a circular motion of her arm, almost spilling her drink—"all this behind."

Webster nods, smiles. "Wally would have said, another level of unreality."

"What? Wally? I don't—"

"Nothing. It's not material."

Laura yawns. "Wallace Stevens. He's Webster's favorite poet. He was very big on unreality."

"Oh. I see. Or I don't. Anyway, Shirly was always his pet. She's younger than most of us and prettier, I suppose. I'm not surprised she would do this for him, but I find it hard to believe he was blackmailing her. From what you say, he doesn't need the money and she would do anything for him anyway. And who would he reveal anything to anyway?"

"What do you mean?"

"She's a widow. She doesn't have any family and she wouldn't give a damn what anybody thought. She's rich and rather wild."

"Doesn't sound likely, then." Webster shrugs. "We don't even know if it's important."

"What do you want me to do?"

"Laura said you usually sponsor a Christmas Eve dance at your club."

"Yes. You want me to invite Allenby?"

"Yes. And the other members of the coven. Especially this Shirly Harris. I want to have Laura and me get the opportunity to get to know her. She'll have to crack. She'll have to be the vulnerable link."

"I don't see how. What pressure can you bring?"

"We'll know more about that after we meet her. And anyway we have to get the negatives first."

"First?"

"Sure, when Allenby gets the invitation, he'll assume that I am going to try to visit his house the night of the dance. So I'll go earlier."

"But then, he'll be there. And LeSsave and the wolves."

The Devil and Webster Daniels

"No. Jack said he goes to see Shirly regularly. And LeSsave always drives him wherever he goes. So it will just be the wolves and I can handle them." Vera shivers. "Can you have the invitation sent by messenger tomorrow?"

Vera nods. "Yes. That's simple enough."

"Fine."

Laura looks at him, shaking her head. "That's what you always say."

The third evening in a row, Webster sits in the Scout pulled off into a clearing in trees a half mile from the entrance to Allenby's estate. It gets cold sitting there and cramped, Webster. Now you know what it must be like for cops on stakeout. Very tiresome.

It is seven-thirty. You are starting to yawn and you've only been here two hours. It's the memory of the thing that gets to you; two nights in a row; ten hours a night; figured he wouldn't go calling after three-thirty. Went back to the bungalow tired, cold, hungry, and testy.

Yawn. You try to keep your eyes from wandering over to the dashboard clock every other minute. Resolve not to look at it for half an hour. Wait. Yawn. Wait.

It surely must be forty-five minutes by now. Five to eight; twenty minutes. Oh, well. But there is someone coming now. A black Mercedes limousine; Allenby's car; LeSsave at the wheel—a hard figure to miss; Allenby in shadow on the far side of the rear seat. Wait ten minutes. Check the paint sprayer filled with mace. Put on the gas mask. Go.

Pulling up the driveway into the turnaround, your headlights catch the forms of the wolves. But they aren't coming. Pull closer. They are chained to their exercise stake. Sit and ponder. Could Allenby have been that confident? Or is he baiting you?

Beat the Devil

There's only one way to find out and you just hate to wonder about that sort of thing, Webster. Take off the gas mask. Around to the back. The back door is locked. Pick the lock this time. Try to be neater. No need to invite LeSsave back for another punch-up if you can help it.

Inside and listen. The silence seems to have the right quality. Take the pencil flash from your bag and straight to Allenby's bedroom. Opening the safes is no real problem, but they are empty. Well, perhaps they just processed them; they'd be in the lab.

Downstairs and in the room; turn the light on; shock. It is completely empty. No equipment, nothing. Just clean stone floor, walls. I'll be damned. Probably, Webster. Turn to go; a note on the inside of the door. Typed.

> Sorry, Mr. Daniels. Not caring to have my equipment ruined a second time, I took the precaution of having LeSsave move it to a more suitable location. If you care to discuss it come up to the library.
> E.A.

What else is there to do, Webster? Two high-backed easy chairs with ottomans are pushed close to the fireplace. The fire is the only light in the room and throws strange peripatetic shadows around the high walls and ceiling. Two small tables beside each chair hold brandy snifters, cigar boxes, ashtrays with wooden matches standing in funnels rising from the center, a bottle of brandy. Allenby sits in one chair. He is wearing a red silk, belted smoking jacket, lounging trousers, slippers. His feet are propped on his ottoman and he is smoking a thin dark cigar.

His voice comes from shadow. "Come in. Do sit down, Mr. Daniels. You must be cold."

Webster sits. "Yes, I am." Picks up the brandy bottle; it is a cognac he has never heard of; the bottle is obviously old and the label is yellowed, dated 1803.

The Devil and Webster Daniels

"You'll find it quite extraordinary. Genuine Napoleon brandy. Something of a rarity these days."

Webster pours a few ounces, warms the snifter with his hands; wonderful aroma; sips, tastes, swallows; silk with a bite. "You're right. It's quite good."

Allenby nods. "The cigars are Haitian and excellent as well. I prefer them to the Cuban. There are both light and dark, since I didn't know your preference."

Webster chooses a blunt dark cigar, bites off the end, and spits the tip in the fire; he lights it slowly, carefully, with one of the long wooden matches; he savors a few puffs, nods. "Excellent. I prefer Monte Cristos, but I wouldn't say they were better." He props his feet on his ottoman, leans back.

Allenby leans forward into half light, stares at Webster's face, leans back. "Your face seems better, if still a little battered-looking."

"It doesn't hurt any more. And I'm used to the look. It's more or less the one I had a few years ago."

Allenby nods. "Yes. I read your memoirs. It's why I started this whole business. I anticipated that it would be interesting."

"Nonsense. You've been here nearly nine months. The book wasn't published until two months ago."

"I was able to read it in manuscript through the auspices of a friend."

"You expect me to believe that?"

"Perhaps not yet. But you will. You ought to be very flattered. So much time, money, effort merely to meet and engage you."

"To what end?"

"To convert or destroy you. Of course, I much prefer the first alternative, but the latter will do if necessary." Such a calm reasonable voice comes from shadow—it should soothe you. Chilly, Webster?

"How nice."

"I suppose you noticed my library on your first tour of the house?"

"Yes. I glanced briefly at the titles."

"Are you a literary man, Mr. Daniels? Your memoirs were excellently written."

"I'm not an academic, but I read."

"The very best way. The academic path is so dry, so unimaginative."

"With some exceptions, I would agree."

"Of course, but the rule remains reasonable." Webster nods. "But to the point. If you read, you must certainly have come across some of the many examples in literature of devil pacts."

"Yes."

"That is what I am proposing to you."

Webster laughs. "And you are supposed to be the devil? Do you really expect me to take this seriously?"

"Not now, perhaps. But read this." He pulls a sheet of parchment from inside his jacket and passes it across. One paragraph; Webster reads it through quickly, then rereads; gives it thought.

> We, the undersigned, agree to a test of wills. Should the party of the first part be victorious, the party of the second part shall surrender his immortal soul at such time as party of the first part shall claim it. Should the party of the second part be victorious, party of the first part shall agree to cease and desist all of his normal activities for one hundred years from end of the contest. Party of the second part shall judge the outcome and his decision shall be final and binding.
>
> Party of the first part   Party of the second part
> Edward Allenby

The Devil and Webster Daniels

"Now you hand me a quill pen and I prick a vein and sign in blood, I suppose."

"If you like. A fountain pen will suffice for me. There's one on the table beside you."

Webster tosses the parchment onto the table. "Be serious, Allenby. What do you want?"

"Just what I say."

"Gibberish. If there was such a being as the devil and you were it"—Webster shrugs—"it's just not plausible that you would be as crude as you are. My face is just one example among your clumsy techniques. Not that I've done a lot better, but I admit my mortality, my frailties."

"You suffer from common ignorance about my powers and my limitations. I do have some extraordinary capabilities, but they are not as broad as is commonly believed. Then, too, I wouldn't want you too apprehensive or I shouldn't think you'd sign."

Webster sighs. "Ridiculous."

"Perhaps you need a few minutes to think it over in private." Allenby's chair is empty and you just know you didn't take your eyes off him, Webster. Look around. He is standing by the door some twenty feet away. "I think I hear LeSsave returning. I must speak to him. I won't be but a few minutes." He is gone and you swear the door didn't open, Webster.

He goes and opens it. Looks down the empty corridor. Goes over the door, walls, floor, and looks up at the ceiling for the trick device that must be there. Mirrors? Projection? Wires? False panels? What did he use, Webster? And you can't find a thing.

Sit in the chair and sip brandy until he returns; and it is excellent. He comes back into the room naturally and walks to his chair.

"What trick did you use?" Allenby merely smiles and shakes his head. Webster shrugs. "Well, it was very good."

Beat the Devil

He picks up the parchment and stares at it. "What if it's a draw?"

Allenby spreads his hands, palms up. "Why, no contest, of course. All bets are off."

"If by cease and desist, you mean you'll clear out and not bother these people again, I'll sign this damn fool thing."

"Certainly. It's much more than that. You'll free the world of my particular brand of what is commonly called evil for a century."

"Flummery." Webster takes the pen and signs; hands it across to Allenby.

"Wonderful. I must tell you, had you not signed, I would have been compelled, much to my regret, to allow LeSsave to kill you."

Webster snorts. "What a performance."

"No, truly, Mr. Daniels. You see, you are something of a threat to me. You are a man with a conscience who does not play by my rules or anyone else's. You hold yourself responsible for your acts and that makes you quite dangerous."

Webster shakes his head, walks out laughing, past the impassive LeSsave, past the chained wolves. Laughing as the Scout pulls out of the drive. But on the road, he gets a funny feeling. Wonders if he should.

The sheriff's place is north of Brewster, just off route 312, and overlooks a finger of Big Rock Reservoir. The dirt road winds into pine and birch and just stops; you sit and look around for a while, trying to find a house; the sheriff's car is next to the Scout where the road ends. Then you notice to your left a particularly dense double row of pines, which camouflage, almost completely, a small trailer. Coming close, you see the windows are masked so no light escapes. It is one of those forty-by-ten or -twelve mobile homes. Knock on the

The Devil and Webster Daniels

door, Webster. When it swings open, there is Barton in white stocking feet, rumpled uniform with the shirttail hanging out. No gun belt. No hat.

"Yes?"

"You could invite me in, Jack. It's cold out here."

He peers at you in the dark. "Webster?"

"Yes."

Swings the door all the way open; lets you in. Stares at your basic-black outfit. "Working clothes?"

Small living room with dim light and old furniture that looks as if it came from the Salvation Army; kitchen alcove and two doors at one end—probably for a bedroom and a bathroom. "Yes. I stay with the old standbys when I get out and around."

"Any luck?"

"Not the kind we wanted." Webster describes his visit, leaving out the pact and the philosophical overtones.

"No negatives and no equipment."

"That's it. It's the equipment that bothers me. He said LeSsave moved it, but I don't believe him. The thing that sticks in the back of my mind—well, was it this Harry Reynolds that reported the incident with the delivery van?"

"Yes." They are sitting in two old overstuffed chairs by an electric space heater. Barton rubs his chin. "I see what you're getting at. Want a beer?"

"Sure."

Barton goes to the half-sized refrigerator, brings back two tall, dark brown glass bottles of Bud. "So maybe there wasn't any delivery at all."

"Oh, there was, but not to Allenby's house."

"Then where? Oh, I see. Shirly Harris?"

"That's what occurred to me. What's the layout of her place? If the things are there, where would they be?"

The sheriff sips his beer. "That's a problem. Her place is

Beat the Devil

nice enough, probably pretty expensive, but it's kind of small for a layout of the size you're looking for."

"How small?"

"It used to be a carriage house on a big estate there, but a few years back the place was sold off in pieces. She bought three acres and the carriage house and had it remodeled. What she really has is kind of a large apartment over a double garage. The garage would be big enough to store the equipment, but not to set it up, not to work in."

Wondering, Webster? Sure. What if they stored it there until you paid your visit, then . . . "Where is her place, Jack?"

"You go over on 312 to 22, jog north a quarter mile, and turn off on the New Fairfield road—it's 39 in Connecticut. Her place is just a mile or so across the line."

"I think I ought to have a look."

"You'll never find it in the dark in this weather. I better lead you over."

"The sooner the better, Jack."

The sheriff finishes his beer, sighs. "It's a hell of a note. No offense, Webster, but fingering marks for a burglar is pretty far off the road for me. Look at this dump. Anybody wants to know if a peace officer around here is honest, all they have to do is look at how he lives. They don't pay anything because they figure you'll do just fine on graft, but it plays hell with an honest man."

There isn't anything you can say to that, Webster, so just nod.

Tail-gating on icy, twisting, narrow roads in the dark is tough, Webster, and the sheriff sets a good pace, and the hills and valleys don't help. Probably feels guilty as hell about it all. And you're glad you have the four-wheel drive and studded snow tires for traction, aren't you, Webster?

The Devil and Webster Daniels

You wouldn't know you had crossed the state line, the terrain and roads are the same; rocky rolling ground, snow covered and heavily wooded; you wouldn't know, but the sheriff's taillights come on and stay; he stops. Foggy breath comes from his mouth as he leans beside your open window, Webster.

"That's her drive there." He indicates a thin blacktop that climbs a small rise to their left. "You can just see a corner of her place next to that clump of trees up there. I, uh . . ." He shakes his head, stomps back to his car.

Webster drives on a few hundred yards, finds a wider drive, pulls onto it, turns around facing out, and parks on a shoulder so the Scout isn't blocking the exit but is out of sight of the main road.

Webster cuts across the wooded ground. Hard going in deep snow and no path. And you're tired by the time you get within sight of the carriage house. There are lights on in the upstairs and a car parked in front of the place. A car with the funny bumps on the roof. And when you're standing by it in the dark, you can just read the legend—Putnam County Sheriff's Office. Chief Deputy Harry Reynolds, no doubt. Makes it a bit more dicey.

Try the side entrance to the garage. Locked. But the kind you can pick in your sleep, Webster. Inside, the pencil flash finds a small sports car and a large van; the kind of truck you used to drive for Railway Express, Webster. Remember the north shore run? Crawling in the back, you find it crammed with the replacement equipment. Sweat in the cold as you have to move gingerly, looking for the tins of film, the negatives. But the only film in the van is the raw stock. Sure. They'd keep the negatives inside the house. Now what, as you creep back out into the cold night? Relock the door with your pick. Stand there wondering what to do. And almost get pinned in the lights of a car turning in the drive that you didn't hear the sound of for the wind. Webster dives flat in the snow by the building.

It is the Mercedes and when it stops, LeSsave gets out. Stands looking around. Looks right at you, Webster. Heart stops. He turns and goes to the door, knocks, is admitted.

Webster sprinting. Through the snow, slip tumbling, falling, up and running high-leg kicks, puff grunt can't breathe, sit in the Scout and gasp, sweat.

Pull closer to the road so you can see down it to the next drive. Wait. Wonder, but it just has to be. Better put on the gas mask and check the sprayer. You've never been a highwayman before, Webster. Well, a fellow ought always be ready to try new experiences. And here comes the van; ponderous and creeping slowly; turns carefully onto the main road going back toward New York State.

Ease the Scout out and follow; tricky as hell, isn't it, Webster, running without lights, trying to stay on the road you can't really see, and trying to gain on the van.

At a curve, you catch the van and coming alongside, snap on the headlights, veer into its side hard to nudge it off the road into the snow. It slides and the nose turns down toward the ditch; the van hesitates and then plunges like a hesitant diver on the high board; it comes to rest with the flat front resting on the far bank of the gully, the tail suspended at a thirty- or forty-degree angle, rear wheels hanging in air and spinning. The rear end of the van, smacking the Scout when it started its turn and descent, sent the Scout in a complete turn, winds up with the nose facing back toward Connecticut.

Webster, paint sprayer in hand, leaps from the Scout, slides down the bank, giggling; LeSsave is fumbling distractedly with the door handle, seems stunned. He looks up and sees a tallish figure in black garb from boots to stocking cap with a gas mask over his face, pointing some large metal tube at him and quivering; seems to be quivering; no . . . laughing.

Webster manages to gasp, "Stand and deliver!", then chokes on his laughter again. But when LeSsave begins coming out of the van, he sprays his face with a long steady stream of ether. LeSsave crumples in the snow. Webster checks to be sure he is out. And he is.

In the van, on the floorboard in front of the passenger seat, is a cardboard box with film tins; several have spilled out; Webster climbs in; awkward position. Pencil flash from his pocket and open a tin; peel a strip of film up and hold the light behind a frame. Negatives.

Count the cans; nine. Wonderful. Stack them in the box and throw the sprayer in on top and get stabbed in the face by approaching headlights. Better move. Struggles out of the cab and falls on his ass, but holds onto the box. The approaching car sprouts whirling cherries on its roof and emits a high-pitched whine; oh shit!

Struggle slip slide up slope and fling the box into the Scout as the car begins to make a sliding turn stop to block the road. Webster in and throwing it in reverse as a man pops from the car and comes to a kneeling position bringing something up from his side and grasping it with both hands. Webster gunning backward, desperately trying to stay on the road and flame and noise and shattering glass spraying around inside the Scout. They're shooting at you again, Webster.

The man is back in the car and coming on, catching you, Webster. Clutch in, decelerating, he is almost on top of you; grinding gear complaint into first and duck your head as you whip around him; two loud reports close by, but no damage, and you are picking up speed as you go back past the van. You can see in the rearview mirror, he is desperately trying to turn around. Makes it. Is coming after you, Webster. Persistent fellow. He must want to be sheriff very badly.

Twisting, rising, falling roads with snow and ice; he gains

Beat the Devil

on you on the straight stretches, but hasn't your traction for the curves, Webster. Swing north on 39, with him close behind. Hug Lake Candlewood going north into high country.

Postage-stamp New England towns dead silent under white coverlet and dark sky; old frame houses, the occasional white frame church with spires like inverted daggers.

Swing east on 37 around the northern tip of Lake Candlewood and he's falling back some on the treacherous roads. Webster rips off the gas mask and flings it aside; makes it easier to see, breathe; your night vision has come back. Coming to route 7, swing south; he's not in sight behind you; he'll have to guess which way you went; but if he guesses right, Webster, route 7 is a reasonable road and he can catch you.

Seems an eternity before you pass New Milford and the bridge on your left; that's another decision for him to make.

Almost no traffic as you hum along past the silent commercial strips decorated with strings of Christmas lights to hide their secular thrust; gas stations, supermarkets, sporting goods stores advertising sales on guns, the odd motel, occasional restaurant. Still no sign of him as you come into Brookfield and the quantity and quality of commerce increases. Shopping centers, diners, real estate offices abound now.

And you're almost to the turn at Caldor Shopping Center now, but whoops! Here he comes. Gaining. Red light ahead and a couple of cars. Webster swings into the empty parking lot and cuts the corner, bumps over a curb and nearly sideswipes a madly honking motorist as he cuts back onto the side road and the deputy's car comes in behind him and the motorist.

It's a break that the motorist is angry, Webster. He's chasing you too and Reynolds can't get around him. Both of them honking wildly and the three cars slipping and skidding at too-high speeds on slick road and pray no one's coming from the other direction. When the cherries start spinning again

The Devil and Webster Daniels

and the siren wails, the motorist pulls over and lets the deputy's car past, but now they are into bends and dips again and Webster starts to pull away once more.

He leans into it with conviction and builds the lead to three quarters of a mile as he approaches the last short straight stretch. Christ they better be home, Webster.

Making the left turn toward the bridge after the straightaway, he is only a little more than a half mile back and coming fast. But you can see he has trouble with the turn and you are climbing the ridge before he gets going again and he can't see you as you go over the rise and two short blocks on, turn right onto a side street. A short way down the block of ranch and Cape Cod houses is a green wood ranch decorated spectacularly with strings of lights and a lighted Nativity scene on the lawn. Turning in the driveway, you can see them sitting in the living room by the lighted tree. The drive dips down steeply and you slide in between the dark green Pinto wagon and a little sports job.

Engine off and grab the sprayer to smash out what remains of the windshield; no bullet holes now. Dump the sprayer back in the box with the mask and tins and leap out holding the box and struggling up the steep drive and scream at the top of your range a primal wail for help—"WARREN!"

He is at the front door; extremely handsome mid-thirtyish-looking young man with a touch, a hint of gray in the full brown hair; some people say he looks a bit like Kevin McCarthy; Warren, Webster's literary agent.

"What on earth is the matter, Webster?"

Breathlessly entering the short hallway, stand in the living room doorway and nod at Richmond. "New York sheriff's deputy is on my tail and I just didn't have anywhere else to go. Can I have been here all evening? It's in a good cause!"

"Of course, you can. Another one of your exotic escapades, I presume."

"Yes."

Warren leads him by the arm gently down a side hall to the bathroom. "Richmond, pour another mug of cocoa, about half full. I thought you'd given up this sort of thing, Webster."

"So did I. Thanks for trusting me, Warren."

"Give me the box; you go in and take a quick shower while I get some dry clothes. How close is he?"

"He couldn't have seen me make the turn into your street, but when he sees the main road doesn't go on through, he'll start checking these side streets." Warren nods and closes the door.

Five minutes of steaming takes the cold out of your bones and almost lets you relax, Webster. Towel dry and try the clothes Warren set just inside the door. The corduroy pants are a little short in the leg, but not bad; the turtle-neck pullover fits nicely as do socks and desert boots.

In the living room, Richmond is tinkering with some chords on the piano; a full head of pure white hair frames a tanned attractive middle-aged face, bright eyes, and a quiet bemused smile. Webster sits on the couch and sips some cocoa. Warren sits in an easy chair from which he can see the road through the picture window.

"I know this is inexcusable, Warren, Richmond, bursting in on you in the middle of the night—"

"Tut, tut, we find it rather exciting, Webster; don't we, Richmond?"

He smiles and plays an ironic half phrase. "Warren is the kind of man who can't resist involvement with his clients. Since you are by far the most dashing man with the agency, it would have been a great blow if you had gone anywhere else." Repeats the half phrase, the smile.

"What did you do, if you can say, Webster?"

Webster chuckles. "Ran a truck into a ditch, gassed the

The Devil and Webster Daniels

driver, pinched the film tins in that box, and led the deputy, who happened along, a high-speed chase over half of Fairfield County."

Warren leans forward toward the window. "I believe your friend just passed by rather slowly. He was using his spotlight on the houses across the road."

"Then we haven't long to wait."

"You're sure you're doing the right thing, Webster?"

"Yes. When I tell you the background, you'll agree."

Warren nods. "Okay, we trust your moral judgments."

"How long have you been here, Webster?"

"Oh, I should say since dinner at eight, how's that?"

"Fine. I believe . . . yes, here he comes." They can see him walking, flashlight in hand down the drive; disappears. Webster lights a cigarette, sips cocoa. Richmond plays the theme from *The Sting*, chuckles.

Reynolds comes back up the drive and around to the door, knocks. Warren answers. "Yes, Officer, what's the difficulty?"

"I'd like to speak to the owner of that International Scout in your drive."

"About what?"

"Criminal charges."

They come into the living room; Reynolds is a stocky, medium-height, dark-haired young man with slightly outsize ears and a crooked nose. "You're Webster Daniels?"

Webster nods up at him. "Yes."

"You own that Scout?"

"No, but I borrowed it from a friend. It's legally in my possession."

"You're under arrest."

"For what?"

"Reckless driving, criminal assault, grand larceny, resisting arrest, and more."

"My, my. When am I supposed to have done all this?"

Beat the Devil

"Within the last hour and a half."

Warren shakes his head. "Quite impossible, Officer, quite impossible. Mr. Daniels is a client of mine and he has been visiting in our home all evening. We had dinner at eight or so and we've been chatting ever since."

Richmond shifts sideways on the piano bench. "Excuse me, but doesn't that patch on your jacket say Sheriff's Deputy, Putnam County, New York?"

"Yes. The crimes took place just inside the New York border."

Richmond smiles. "But my good man, you're in Fairfield County, Connecticut, now. Aside from the fact that your story is preposterous and quite impossible, you haven't a chimera of jurisdiction here. You can't arrest anyone in this state, even if your suspicions were more than the obvious moonshine that they are."

Reynolds looks hesitant. "Come on, Daniels. You can't get away with it."

Webster shakes his head. "I haven't the faintest notion what you're talking about."

Warren touches him on the elbow. "I think it's best if you leave now."

Reynolds looks at all of them; sees calm unruffled expressions; grimaces. "You'll pay, Daniels." Walks out angrily, but outside they can see his shoulders slump as he plods toward the car. Richmond plays the melody line of "The Party's Over"; they all laugh. Reynolds pulls down the street a house or two and parks.

"Looks like he's going to wait for you to leave. You'll stay the night, of course."

"If you don't mind."

"Of course we don't."

"I need to make a couple of phone calls, if I may?"

"Certainly. This way."

The Devil and Webster Daniels

They stay up until nearly dawn; Richmond playing Cole Porter and regaling them with stories of his experiences on professional tours; Webster tells them a little about this adventure; Warren tells them some of the latest literary anecdotes and tries to persuade Webster to try his hand at a novel. While they talk, Webster burns the negatives.

In the afternoon, after sleep and late breakfast, Jack Barton shows up to escort Webster back. They make a cavalcade; Webster in the Scout, Barton behind him, and Reynolds, who has slept in his car, bringing up the rear.

Back at the bungalow, Barton comes in for coffee. Laura shakes her head.

"Look at you. I go nearly out of my head worrying about you and you come prancing in like you've been at nothing more dangerous than a schoolboy larking about in his tree house."

Webster looks surprised. "I told you on the phone, this morning, that everything was under control."

Laura nods. "You always think so. If you didn't have the reflexes of a cat—"

"But I do."

"Yes, but you needn't live on them. You could build a little more margin of safety."

"Nonsense, then it wouldn't be any fun. And you know it."

The sheriff clears his throat. "Excuse me, but speaking of having things under control, well, I'm real glad you got the negatives and have kinda put out the fire we spoke about, but I still got a problem with that Harris woman. DA's going to impanel a grand jury the middle of January. I was wondering if you got any ideas about that."

Laura laughs. "Don't you worry your head, Sheriff. Webster is in charge. He won't let you down."

Beat the Devil

Webster bows, smiles. "Jack, it won't ever get to a grand jury. I promise you."

Barton looks at him a moment, sighs. "I have to admit you're an amazing man," turns to Laura, "no offense, ma'am. And I'll be very grateful if you can pull this whole thing off. But the fact remains, until you showed up—you and Allenby —I had a very peaceful, prosperous county. I feel too old for this kind of, uh, excitement. Nothing personal, but I have to admit I'll be glad to see the last of you."

Webster laughs. "I'd feel very uncomfortable if you didn't feel that way, Jack. When I don't feel like an outlaw, I'm unhappy. I guess I just don't have the nature of a citizen."

"Yeah, that's the trouble. You're doing something I think needs doing, but you'd be just as big a wizard doing something I couldn't keep on my conscience."

The sheriff drives them into Brewster to the railroad station; stays with them until they board a late train for the city; Webster takes the prints along in a sack, has to see a man about a comedy.

Christmas Eve at the country club. Four hundred guests from Putnam, Westchester, Fairfield counties; evening gowns and tuxedos; Puerto Rican help are in this year; small jazz combo somewhat better than the crowd deserves; buffet dinner with roast beef, turkey, ham, salads, soups, seafood, desserts—enough food to feed four hundred people for three days; the ballroom decorated in primary colors and five bars surrounding it on every side. Laura and Webster dancing slow.

"Dear Webster, even with that ugly face, you're the handsomest man here." Their outfits are gold crushed velvet.

"Only here?"

"Greedy."

"It's just that I need to be truly spectacular or people will

The Devil and Webster Daniels

wonder what a beautiful woman like you is doing with a mug like me."

"Sneaky, too. You always were good at sliding out from under. If you weren't so good at compliments, it wouldn't work. Or"—Laura presses close—"if you weren't so good in—"

Webster puts a hand over her mouth. "Hush. You'll shock the citizenry." Laura licks the palm of his hand. "Don't be sexy. At least not here where we can't—"

"Who says we can't?"

He laughs. "You always did have a thing for dance floors. I remember the ballroom at the Drake Hotel."

"So do I."

"Has Vera introduced you to Shirly Harris, yet?"

"Yes. Very nice if you like short blondes with disproportionate boobs. You never said you did, though."

"Never said I didn't either." Laura kicks his shin. "But of course I don't, love."

"Mmmm."

"All right, I'm going to find Allenby. When you see us take our drinks to the lounge, you know what to do."

"Have I ever failed you, Webster?"

"No."

Webster wanders through and around the crowd, nodding politely to people he's been introduced to; usually he can't remember their names. Allenby is at the bar nearest the door, farthest from the dancing. He is standing alone, drinking what appears to be scotch. He nods as Webster approaches, motions the barman to bring another drink.

"Scotch, I believe, Mr. Daniels."

"Usually is. On the rocks."

"I must compliment you, Daniels."

"Yes?"

"That was a rather magnificent recovery and performance the other evening. I thought I had disconcerted you enough that you wouldn't start thinking again, let alone acting, for several days."

Webster bows slightly. "Thank you."

"I've underestimated you three times. I won't do it again."

"Too bad. I suppose I'll actually have to start extending myself, then."

Allenby smiles, but those black burning eyes have no warmth. "It comes from having dealt too long with inferior types. You begin to forget how to deal with high-quality players." Webster motions the barman for new drinks.

"Let's take these somewhere quiet. I hate to talk with all this noise." Allenby nods and they take their drinks and slip out the door. Down the hall and to the right is a series of small lounges which are actually one long room with archways breaking it up into conversation areas. They sit in matching chairs drawn up to a small table; one lamp illuminates the area; an arch is at Allenby's back.

"So, where do we stand?"

Allenby frowns. "You can't believe it's over. There are so many loose ends. I admit your coup of the other night has presented me with a major setback, but I'm not beaten yet. Not by any means."

"Hmmmm."

Now Allenby looks disturbed; you could almost say frightened, couldn't you, Webster? "You can't render a judgment at this point."

"Why not? I didn't see any subclauses in that contract. No time limit, no specifics. Just my judgment, final and binding."

"But it was obvious that the agreement was based on honor. That I assumed you were a man with honor."

"What if the assumption was wrong?" Allenby just stares at him. "I can make a judgment of my victory at any point under any circumstances and you're done. I've already won, Allenby."

The Devil and Webster Daniels

"A cheap trick. I thought you had better than that in you."

"That's right. It wasn't honor you counted on; it was pride. My ego."

"Yes."

Webster smiles. "You were right of course. I make no judgment at this point."

Allenby relaxes, lifts his glass. "To your well-deserved pride, Mr. Daniels."

Webster drinks. "Do you still maintain this fiction that you came here solely to get at me?"

"It's not a fiction."

"You had, have, no interest in any of your other, mmm, victims?"

"Of course not. They are merely tools."

"All the recruiting, setting up the coven, the filming, the blackmail—all this to get at me? All the members of the coven, they're just all tools?"

"Of course. You've met the silly wretches. Do you have such a low opinion of me as to think I'd be interested in them? Now, your woman, Laura, would be quite another matter."

Webster leans forward, taps him on the knee. "Don't even think about it, Allenby. That way lies death." He sits back. "But what about this, uh, Harris? Vera tells us you have a special thing with her."

Allenby yawns. "The worst of the lot. I have to pamper her vanity constantly. She's possessive with me; can you imagine such a ridiculous idea? As if such as she could possess me." He shrugs. "I only bother with her because of her connection with the deputy. I foresaw that the sheriff might be a problem—" He stops speaking, stares at Webster's grin. "What am I saying—"

"Enough, you bastard!" A blond banshee flings herself upon Allenby, pummeling his face and head with her fists and they tumble to the floor. He manages to pull partially away before Webster can move, draws back a fist and smashes the woman in the mouth; her head snaps back hard; she covers her face, but blood seeps out between her hands; she cries. Allenby struggles to his feet as Laura and Webster kneel beside the woman.

They help her to her feet; Laura leads her away to the rest room for first aid. Allenby is straightening his jacket, tie, and shirt which were rumpled during the scuffle. Webster eyes him coldly.

"Another not especially impressive performance for you, Allenby."

His stare is every bit as cold as yours, Webster; and he manages to look harder than you've seen him before; hardly seems possible.

"It's not over yet, Daniels."

"No. Not quite."

He is gone; you stare at the spot of blood on the carpet; that's a bad dude when crossed. Finish your drink, Webster, and wait for Laura.

She returns in fifteen minutes, sits next to you, hands you a fresh drink. She holds her glass close to yours and you touch them, small click. "To Webster triumphant."

He grins. "My friends what can I say but I'll drink to that?"

"She's not hurt badly. Physically, anyway. Her boyfriend, the deputy, was outside. He's taking her home."

"Did you mention Barton?"

Laura nods. "She's agreed to exonerate the sheriff if he won't prosecute her. She's going to see him tomorrow."

Back in the ballroom the party goes on as if nothing has happened, nothing changed. Perhaps it hasn't.

Vera tells them that she has told all the other members of the coven that Allenby's hold on them is gone. They had thanked her profusely as she thanks Webster; she has extracted pledges of another quarter of a million dollars for Amnesty, International.

Laura and Webster dance a while, have a few drinks, laugh. When they get back to the bungalow, their need is strong, their bodies right, but afterward she seems distant again.

Forty-degree weather and sun in mid-January; the kind of climate anachronism that can make you feel it's almost spring, when there's really a couple more months of winter; slip on a windbreaker and go for a drive. Laura and Webster in the blueberry coupe. Driving around Lake Candlewood on the route he took when pursued.

"How fast did you say you were driving?"

"Fifty and sixty."

"Icy roads too."

"Yes, it was a little hairy here and there." Laura shivers. "Looks worse in daylight, love."

"Sometimes I really worry about you, Webster. I think you like to flirt with . . . death."

Webster is startled. "Whatever gave you an idea like that, Laura?"

She laughs. "I don't know. Must have come to me in a dream."

They go north on route 7; winding through foothills, forest; the Housatonic is usually in sight, winding with them. They drive in silence as Webster chews his mustache. You ought to think that one over, Webster.

"Maybe you're right. I never think about it that way. It's just that the danger, the excitement make me feel alive. Outwitting somebody . . . I'm not an artist, a musician, a writer—Warren to the contrary—and business bores me. What else is there? Politics? Not an open option for me."

"I know. But what will you do after this is over? You can't keep doing this kind of thing always."

Webster shrugs. "I'll worry about that at the right time."

They have come back down route 45 to New Preston; he swings through the tiny town—post office, two grocery stores, a couple of gas stations, hardware store, drugstore—takes the winding road around Lake Waramaug; on the western edge is a state park and camp grounds. Webster pulls into the deserted grounds, parks by the water's edge. Mid-afternoon sun is hard and not warm, seems to break on the chill blue surface of the water. Picnic lunch in the front seat. Hot thermos of tea, a loaf of crusty bread, three kinds of sharp cheese, green and ripe olives, sweet pickles, hot peppers, half bottle of sturdy Chianti.

"Do you believe he's the devil?"

"Allenby?"

"Yes."

"Nonsense, love. You have to believe in God to believe in the devil. You know me, love; I don't believe in either one."

"You're sure that was a trick he pulled that night?"

"Had to be."

"Had to be?"

"Sure, unless he's a psychic with the power to transpose matter, which I don't buy for a minute."

"And you're not worried about that . . . that pact you agreed to?"

"No. My immortal soul? Hogwash. I just think it's all some elaborate ploy on his part."

"To what end?"

"I don't know. He wants something from me, but I can't see what it is."

"Mmmm. The man *is* evil, Webster. I'll never forget the day we went to his house. And you can feel it, just feel . . . bad things coming from him."

The Devil and Webster Daniels

"I'll admit he's a nasty character, not an ideal dinner companion, but evil, the devil? That's a little far out for my taste."

"You're probably right."

Sipping the hot tea, the picnic basket returned to the back seat, they relax and watch wind make breakers on the lake, sun squeeze liquid gold through pine branches.

Laura leans against him, head on his chest; under the windbreaker she wears a loose red sweater, wool slacks.

"Webster." She is gently rubbing the inside of his thigh.

"I like that . . . tone of voice." He kisses her hair, forehead, and slips a hand under her sweater; warm smooth skin.

"I haven't made love in a car seat since I was a high school student." She has unzipped his trousers.

"Me . . . either." They giggle as they shed their slacks and twist-squirm to find a position on the narrow bench seat. It is slow and sweet. Has humor.

"All we need now is some clown who gets his jollies from coitus interruptus . . . be just like . . . being a kid . . . again."

Slow-ride tongues touch warm gentle pleasure; love. Her eyes are so green, deep green, you've never seen any like them, Webster. Never even dreamed any like them.

"Oh . . . this is . . . how . . . we . . . no holding back, Webster. . . . I can't stand not . . . to give . . . all."

Moist eyes, but they are both happy. Seems like they ride forever. The car might be a space ship and they frozen in deep space; they would not care. There is only them. Riding. Then rising, hold tight, passing through one another into a dimension of joy.

Lay spent together. Not thinking. Listening to their breathing. Feeling their bodies, their selves together.

He brushes back a strand of her long dark hair that sweat plastered to her forehead. Hands her the cigarette.

Beat the Devil

Webster laughs. "I wonder if this is the real reason America worships cars."

Laura laughs too. "I know it was when I was sixteen." Passes the cigarette back to him. "I didn't like the hot rods. Whenever one would squeal tires going by, I used to shout, 'Getting any lately?' "

The sun is dropping away fast. Clothed, warm, they huddle in each other's arms. They share the last of the tea, lukewarm now, and kill the wine. They have silence together.

They ride south on route 7 again; dusk now and cold; you can't pretend it's spring any more. Laura drives now and Webster hums tuneless, absent-minded, relaxed.

"Webster."

"Now, that tone of voice I'm not crazy about." She slaps him on the thigh.

"I've had an offer."

"I shouldn't wonder, beautiful woman like you."

"Webster, be serious."

"Must I?" She nods. "Okay. An offer?"

"You remember Johanna Green?"

"The editor of *Feminist?* Did the story on us?"

"That's her. She wants me to be an international correspondent for them. Write a monthly article on the movement in Europe."

"Do you want to?"

"I think I want to give it a try. I want to see if I can do something that won't be easy for me."

Webster shrugs. "Sure. I can see that."

"The thing is . . . it may not make any sense, but I feel like I have to do by myself for a while. Somehow, if I didn't, I would feel like I was playing at it."

The Devil and Webster Daniels

Webster smiles. "That's not very logical, but I'm afraid I can understand that too."

They share a different kind of silence for a few miles; Webster lights cigarettes for them.

"Where will you go?"

"Johanna wants me to use Paris as a base. I'll be traveling a lot."

"I guess you better do it. Like you said, it's got to be giving all with us. I don't think we would ever be any good at an arrangement."

"It's not forever. Just until I get my feet on the ground."

Webster smiles his crooked grin. "That's right. Nothing is forever."

They meet Warren in the cocktail lounge where Richmond plays. They have drinks; Warren has ginger ale. Richmond plays Cole Porter for them because Webster likes him so well.

Richmond Gell; "Making Whoopee."

The end of January; Laura is in the city for conferences with Johanna Green; Webster alone and the weather mild for this time of year. Webster waits. He is learning patience.

Once, Jack Barton comes around. The good plain face pensive, the manner gentle. They sip bourbon in the early afternoon. Webster keeps a fire in the bungalow and they warm their feet.

"The Harris woman recanted her charges to the grand jury yesterday. I'm being exonerated."

"That's good news."

"I fired Harry Reynolds."

"Seems reasonable."

"Hated to do it. He was a good deputy until he lost his head over that woman."

"Still . . ."

"Yeah, I can't have a chief deputy that goes that far over the line." He shifts uncomfortably in his chair, takes a swallow of whisky. He is trying to figure how to say something, Webster. "I owe a lot to you, Webster. If it hadn't been for you, I might be in a fair way to go to jail."

Webster smiles, but gently—does not want to be smug with the sheriff. "It was my pleasure, Jack. And I owed it to you."

"The thing is . . . well, the, uh, coven is sort of broken up. . . . It seems like you've put out the fire that we talked about and I was wondering . . ." His face flushes and he can't go on, Webster.

"You wonder why I don't pack up and leave your county in peace, but you don't want to say that because it sounds ungracious."

He nods. "Something like that. I don't think I'm going to run for re-election this fall, but I'd like to have a nice quiet year to end my term. I could do without any more special thrills."

"I would, Jack, but it's not over."

He nods again. "I was afraid you'd say that. Any idea how long it's going to take?"

"Another month, month and a half. I'm having some work done in the city that should resolve it."

"Are there going to be any more, uh, flames?"

"I don't honestly know. I don't think so, but that's not based on any solid knowledge."

"Let me know if you need any help or if you see something coming."

"Sure."

The beginning of February; snow returns in several storms the first week; Webster waits alone. Once, he returns from a late night walk to find Allenby sitting by the fire in the bungalow. The same hard, burning black eyes without warmth. He is dressed casually, seems relaxed, has helped himself to a glass of whisky. Webster sits and they stare at each other for a few minutes without speaking.

Webster is smug with him. "Is the game losing its amusement value?"

"No. I'll admit you disconcerted me several times. You've done very well, Webster."

"I see. We're on a first-name basis now."

"Why not?"

"All right, Edward." Hard to say, isn't it, Webster? A little like first-naming Hitler or Stalin? The Adolph sticks in the throat.

"I needed to see you. I need to know . . . if you understand . . . if you realize the position?"

"I think I do."

He twirls the glass and the fire colors the amber fluid, moves in it. "If you had to put a name to your philosophy, Webster, what would the name be?"

He shrugs. "Existentialism, I suppose. If you need a name."

"Are you familiar with Camus, Sartre?"

"Sure."

"You know Camus' essay, 'The Myth of Sisyphus'?"

"Yes."

"Think of yourself, in our little game, as Sisyphus and of me as the rock that you must push up the hill over and over again. You have pushed me up the hill several times and now I am rolling downhill again. You stand at the top preparing to descend and push me up again. This, you remember, is the one time, says Camus, in the repetitive process, the one time that Sisyphus can think, feel, exist. The rest of the time, he—you are chained to the process."

"I remember he said that. I said I was familiar with Camus and Sartre. I didn't say that I swallowed them whole."

"Of course not. I am merely using his analogy, but it is at this point that we change it. You believe that you are only going to have to push me up that hill this one last time, that this time I will roll over the top and disappear. Is that correct?"

"Yes."

"I believe that when you try to push me this time I will be too heavy, will roll back on you, will crush you. I not only believe it, I know it, I welcome it. I anticipate it with pleasure."

"So?"

"The point is, this is your special time to reflect."

"And yours."

"Not really. I'm more like the rock than you think. I am more in the nature of a hard fact. I do what I do. I do not think about it. The only reason that I am fully conversant with man's philosophical musings is that I need to be able to communicate with some men in their terms. I am bound by one code only. When I enter into the kind of contest we have contracted for, I must be sure that you, my opponent, understand exactly what is involved. You must realize that the only way you can win is to convince me that you have won. Technically, the pact says you can win just by saying so, but you know that you can never believe you have won unless I do. And my will is indomitable, yours is not."

"You say."

"I do indeed, Webster. The other thing you must realize is that I can use any means. You are restricted by your conscience. I am not. I can and will do anything to crush you."

"What I think, Allenby, excuse me, Edward, is that you are a pretentious bore. I don't pretend to know why you have gone through all these elaborate machinations and I don't know that I much care. But you might as well give up this philosophical monologue, there is no way you will convince me that you are the devil. As the king would say, 'We are not amused.'"

"I think you know what I am talking about. You are artful at the sophisticated skeptical pose. You wear your cynicism well."

Webster yawns. Allenby has ceased to interest him. He wishes Laura was back. After a time, he goes and gets a drink; proceeds about the bungalow as if he were alone, ignores Allenby; looks up some time later—and he is gone. Didn't hear the door open or close, but then it's not a very noisy door.

The Rolling Stones; "Sympathy for the Devil."

CHAPTER VI

The Devil's Game

Blue haze later afternoon mid-February; cold mountain air is like a body stocking, an extra garment you wear. Webster paces the board platform of the Brewster railway station, waits for the first commuter train; Laura is coming back. Old snow is crusted at the edges of the platform; farther in it mingles with some slush, makes footing treacherous; Webster's old suede desert boots are acquiring a dark gravy of the mixture he thinks of as snudge. He wears a dark blue three-quarter-length navy-surplus coat, stocking cap pulled low on his forehead; looks like a local laborer; hands in pockets he paces.

Webster waits. Commuter trains come and go; after the

The Devil and Webster Daniels

first one they come closer together until there is one every few minutes; that goes on for a while; they start to thin again. Webster waits. No dark-haired woman escapes his glance, but where is Laura? The commuter rush is over; now the trains will run only every half hour.

Webster in a pay phone booth. Calls her hotel. No, Ms. Deveraux checked out at three o'clock; the bell captain ordered a taxi to take her to Grand Central. But where is Laura?

No response at the offices of *Feminist*; they would be closed and no one working late on a Friday. The home phone of Johanna Green gets only her answering service: Ms. Green is out of town for the weekend and cannot be reached.

He eats a hurried unsatisfactory supper in the diner half a block from the train station, takes a large cup of coffee back with him. Webster waits. Greets the half hourly, then hourly trains with diminished expectation.

Webster's visible breath is his only companion pacing the board platform. There are seldom sounds except the wind and his own footsteps. The coffee has not kept him warm long; the body-stocking cold seems under the skin now, a kind of inner rather than outer garment; still the deeper chill setting in is not climatic. Where is Laura? Webster waits.

At 1 A.M., the last train secretes less than a dozen passengers like a furtive and shameful glandular overfunction discharge best done quickly and under cover of darkness.

Webster watches each passenger open the door to pass through the station; they are illuminated momentarily by fleeing light; none is Laura.

Webster leans against the wall of the station; the steep wooded slope across the tracks is only shadow now, except for a few lights in the random houses; Webster worries. It is not like Laura; she doesn't fail to show without calling; of course she could have decided at the last minute to go

The Devil's Game

for the weekend with Johanna Green. But why wouldn't she call?

The blueberry coupe is cold and it takes long minutes to warm it up. Webster drives slowly back to the bungalow. Inside, he warms himself by the fire with cognac in coffee. You have fears you don't want to admit, don't you, Webster? As if by metaphysical alchemy, to admit a fear brings the dread to pass, makes it real. And what if you call out the police for a search and Laura calls up to say she's spending the weekend some place else; for twentieth-century Western man, the ultimate sin is to make a fool of yourself; and you're nobody's fool, are you, Webster?

Still, he phones Jack Barton; he recommends they wait until morning and try to get ahold of Ms. Green; Webster agrees reluctantly. Sleeps fitfully.

In the morning, his driving is so jerky and erratic that he slides into old snowdrifts twice, gets stuck, takes half an hour to get free both times. Get a grip on yourself, Webster.

It is ten-thirty when he gets to Barton's trailer. The sheriff is dressed and sitting by his phone; he offers Webster instant coffee and motions him to sit.

"Bit late."

"I got stuck in the snow a couple times."

"Nervous driving?"

"Nervous period."

Barton nods. "Well, I wish I could ease your mind some, but I can't. I called a friend of mine in missing persons department of the city police. He located this Green woman out on Long Island. She said as far as she knew, Laura hadn't changed her plans and was intending to come back up here."

Webster sighs. "Now what?"

"Lieutenant Levy, that's my friend, is going to get some

pictures of Laura through that magazine. The Green woman agreed to call somebody in the city to open up a file and get some pictures they have of Laura from the article they did on you two."

"And?"

"Then they have to try to run down the conductors who were on last night's trains and see if she ever got on one."

"How long will that take?"

"Hard telling. That's a fair number of conductors and most of them might be off today and tomorrow. Could take a while to track them down."

Webster sips bitter coffee black. "I'm not a real good one for this kind of waiting."

Barton passes a hand across his chin. "I kind of figured you might be a man to want to move on something like this. Tell you what I thought we might do. I got some things to be doing, some moving around. I told Dave—that's Lieutenant Levy—to call here whenever he gets any information. Why don't you stay here and take the calls? Give you something to do."

"I guess so."

"I scotch-taped a schedule to the desk top so you can see how many trains there were. Cross them out as they're eliminated."

"What for? Busy work?"

"Something like that."

Webster snorts. "You don't have to hold my hand, Sheriff. I'm a big grown-up boy."

Barton's face crinkles in a gentle half-sad smile. "I know, Webster. But the pressure's going to be tough until we find her. Even for a man like you, used to pressure. You don't have to pose with me, son. It's written all over your face. I can tell. I've read that kind of writing more than a few times."

The Devil's Game

Webster flushes. "Sorry, Jack. I *am* edgy. You know what I'm afraid . . ."

"Yeah, I know. Can't jump that way yet, but it's why I'm having the calls come here rather than to the office or over the radio." He gets up, goes and puts on his Stetson and mackinaw. "There's some of what I eat in the refrigerator and the cupboards. Don't know as you could exactly call it food, but if you get hungry it'll stuff the hole in your stomach."

"Thanks, Jack. I'm not very hungry."

Barton nods. "I know. I'll check back every hour or so."

"Okay."

After he is gone, restless Webster can't resist the professional's urge to prowl. The cupboards contain canned soups, chili, one-dish meals like ravioli; the refrigerator has some cold packaged meat, bread, cheese, beer; the kind of solitary diet you remember well, Webster.

The bedroom has a small double bed, one chair, and lamp, a small dresser without many clothes, and a truly tiny closet with three extra uniforms and one plain blue suit, two dark ties. The bed's headboard is a bookshelf stuffed with paperbacks and two clothbound volumes: *Diamonds Are a Boy's Best Friend* and *The Plantain Season;* the paperbacks are mostly novels ranging from *Winds of War* to *Bitter Chocolates.*

He goes back to the sitting room, lies on the couch, smokes; Webster waits. Hard. Fears the phone won't ring. Fears it will.

At one, he makes a bowl of chili, opens a beer. If he was still an eighteen-year-old fraternity boy, he could light farts all afternoon to amuse himself.

At two, Levy calls; two trains have been eliminated; Webster draws a blue line through each one on the schedule. Busy work. The rest of the afternoon and on into the evening he is taking calls from Levy and Barton; blue lines begin to dominate the schedule. For supper he has a bologna sandwich with lots of tabasco so you know there's something there to taste; glass of milk; oreo cookies; remembered diet.

At nine, Barton returns. "Nothing too helpful yet, Webster?"

"Just more blue lines. I don't see how they're helpful. Or even very interesting."

"How many trains left to go?"

"Five in the commuter rush time, six later on."

"Uh-huh. Dave's working pretty fast. You eaten?"

"I guess that's what it was."

Barton laughs. "I know. I keep telling myself I ought to learn to cook proper. Maybe I'll have a chance after I retire." He goes into the small kitchen, begins rummaging in the cupboards. "Think I'd like to go to one of these fancy schools. *Cordon Bleu* or some such."

"French cooking is beautiful, but it'll give you the gout in short order."

"Nah, not me. That's a rich man's disease. Besides I don't exactly see how it could do me any more harm than this junk." He emerges from the kitchen with a plate of ravioli, a couple slices of buttered bread, and a beer. He eats methodically and without much relish. "How you holding up?"

"Just barely."

"I know." Barton looks at him thoughtfully. "I've never been married, never been tied to one person." Resumes chewing. Swigs beer. "Sometimes I think that's been a mistake. I see people in trouble and, even then, it seems to make them more . . . what's the word I want?"

"Human?"

"That'll do. More human to care so much. Even if the price sometimes is a whole bunch of worry and pain." Webster nods; there isn't much to say to that; just agree.

The Devil's Game

The phone rings; Webster starts for it, but Barton puts down his food, motions him back; answers it sitting at the small desk.

"Sheriff Jack Barton." Listens. "Hi, Dave. How you doing for me?" Listens with an occasional grunt; picks up a pen and starts scratching notes on a pad of paper.

Listens some more. "Okay, Dave. I sure appreciate the fast work. Looks like we'll have to follow it up from this end. Keep a lid on it if you can?" Listens. "Right. Thanks a lot, Dave. I really appreciate it." He hangs up. Tears off the sheet. Turns to face Webster. "She got on the four-oh-five, the conductor remembered her clearly because he thought he knew her from the newspapers or television. Kept looking at her thinking maybe she was a movie star whose name he ought to remember. That's why he noticed she got off at Katonah and got into a black sedan driven by a man who he can't really describe. That's all he knows."

"It's enough. Ten to one, that sedan was a Mercedes."

"I wouldn't bet on it either way. She wouldn't happen to know anybody around Katonah, would she?"

"Yes. Lily Rowan has a place there, but she doesn't use it except in the summer. And Laura wouldn't go there and not call." Webster moves.

"Where you heading?"

"I have to see a man about a Mercedes."

"That's a little too quick on the draw."

"I don't think so, Sheriff."

"If you're going, I'd better come with you."

"I can handle it better alone."

"Sure thing, son. And in the mood you're in, I'd have to spend the next few months cleaning up corpses. I'd hate to have to lock you up, Webster, but I will if I think it's necessary."

"If you're coming, let's go."

The Devil and Webster Daniels

The sheriff follows the blueberry coupe. Webster sets a rapid pace even on the icy roads. His driving is controlled anger now. No nerves.

And Allenby laughs at them; takes them on a complete tour of the house and grounds; can account for the time period in question for both himself and LeSsave. And always he is smirking at you, Webster; letting his eyes tell you that he has her. Outside, Barton lectures you standing in the cold by the cars.

"Don't even think about it, Webster. If he's got her, we'll be able to trace it; we'll find her."

"How? And how soon?"

"It'll take some time. I won't lie to you about that, but we'll get it done. I don't want to have to lock you up, but I'm going to put twenty-four-hour surveillance on you and on this place and, if you try to come in here, I'll pull you in and throw away the key. I'm not going to have any murders in my county, son. Not now. Not any way."

"Not even Laura's?"

"Don't strike me as reasonable, son. That fellow isn't after that. He doesn't do it that way."

"You better be right, Sheriff."

Barton gives his gentle, half-sad smile again. "I know, Webster. I know."

In the bungalow, the phone is ringing. When Webster answers it, he hears a metallic click and hum, then Laura's voice, hesitant, a query, "Webster? . . ." Then the click and hum again, then her voice again. "Webster? . . ." Click, hum. "Webster? . . ." Click, hum. "Webster? . . ." Click, hum. "Webster? . . ." Webster hangs up.

Webster in a helpless rage; picks a glass off the bar and hurls it into the fireplace; grabs the poker and beats it out of shape on the brick hearth, drops it; sits.

After a time, forlornly walks through the bungalow, checking all the rooms. Perhaps he will find her in one.

Later, he cleans up the broken glass, tries to bend the poker back into shape. He decides to go to bed; he will try to think about it in the morning.

As he is undressing, the phone rings. He answers it and hears a voice, distant, as if speaking through a tube; it might be Allenby's; it might not. "She is quite beautiful. The golden skin is exquisite, so silken to the touch . . . magnificent body, so firm yet so yielding . . . but I do not need to tell you. You have lain between those lovely legs so often. As others now will." The connection is cut. The dial tone hums in his ear.

He lays on the bed and smokes; he cannot think; he does not try to sleep. The phone calls come every two hours. Some have short sentences in Laura's voice, repeated until he hangs up.

"Webster, please help me. . . . Webster, please help me. . . . Webster, please help me. . . ."

Some have short speeches implying that the speaker is enjoying Laura's body. That their "large friend whose apparatus is proportionate to the rest of his physique" is enjoying Laura's body. That "our animal friends" have a taste for women, enjoy Laura's body. Describing the possible combinations up to and including an accommodation of all five.

Some have just sounds, heavy breathing, sobs and moans that could be Laura and could be from pain or pleasure or both.

He does not eat or drink or sleep. Just smokes and waits. The calls stop at nine in the morning. By noon, he has fallen asleep.

He is awakened by Barton in early evening; they go into the living room; Barton shows him a package that was outside the bungalow door. It is a manila envelope; ripping it open,

Webster finds photographs; black and white, several angles of a dark-haired woman and a huge blond man; the focus is slightly blurred and you cannot see all of the man or woman or their faces. It might be Laura and LeSsave; might not.

Webster explains to the sheriff about the phone calls. They both sit in silence for a long time. Finally, Barton stands up.

"You wait here, Webster. I'll be back in less than an hour."

He comes back in forty-five minutes; he sits in a chair with an oilskin package in his lap; stares at Webster without speaking for several minutes. Then sighs.

"I'm doing something I never thought I would. I've called off the surveillance of you and of Allenby's place." He leans over and puts the package in Webster's lap. Open it, Webster. There is a blue-black automatic pistol, three full clips, and a box of shells.

"You know how to use one of those?"

"Yes. I was on the rifle team in high school and I competed in handgun matches."

Barton nods. "That's a .32 with a nine shot clip; put one in the chamber and you get ten rounds. It's a gun I took off a drunk seven, eight years ago. Untraceable." He stands up. "After I walk out that door, I've never seen it. And you're on your own. If you mess it up, I can't protect you." Webster nods and Barton walks out the door.

Webster in basic black in the blueberry coupe and wondering. Is this what Allenby wants? Does it matter? He must free Laura. Doesn't matter what it costs.

He stops just short of the entrance and takes out the pistol; he inserts a cartridge in the chamber, eases off the hammer, puts in the full clip; slides the pistol back into his jacket pocket.

In the driveway and as he comes to a stop by the house,

LeSsave, with the wolves on leashes, comes around the back corner. Webster shuts off the engine, waits. When they are within ten feet, he swings open the car door, steps out with the pistol in his hand. LeSsave stops, stares at him. Webster braces his arm on the door and sights. Flame and roar and a cut-short yelp and snarling, flame and roar, flame and roar, flame and roar, flame and roar, flame and roar, flame and roar. Webster snaps out the partially spent clip, snaps in a new full one. LeSsave stares at him, stunned; at his feet the bodies of the wolves lay closely grouped, ripped by the bullets, staining the snow and steaming as heat escapes. Webster lifts the barrel and points at LeSsave's head; clicks back the hammer.

"You can join them if you want to. Otherwise, take me to your master."

"Right here, Webster." Allenby is at his side. Webster shifts so that he can cover both of them. Allenby looks down at the torn bodies. "That I suppose was a demonstration of your willingness to kill to effect the return of Laura."

"That and something of a satisfaction."

"Yes, I've noticed you don't care for wolves."

"Where is she?"

"Come now, Webster. You don't really think this is going to work, do you?"

Webster shrugs. "Whether it works or not, it's LeSsave next, then you."

"But if you do kill us without getting Laura back, what happens to her?"

"Maybe I'll find her, maybe I won't, but you've pushed too hard, Allenby. I'm beyond that kind of calculation now. It's a simple either/or proposition."

"And you're willing to go to prison for life?"

"If I have to. It's not likely I will have to. I checked on you. Your background, citizenship, etc., are pretty well invisible. Officially you're something of a cipher. If I kill you and get rid of the body neatly—and I assume I could find some acid in the basement—I don't suppose anyone will put the pieces together. Sheriff Barton won't. So who will?"

Allenby is shaking his head admiringly. "Very nice try, Webster. An estimable attempt. Nicely thought out and nicely played. But I know you better than that. You're just not a violent—" Webster turns, snaps three shots in rapid succession, and LeSsave goes down. He moans and holds his stomach.

"You think I value your lives more highly than those wolves?" Webster shakes his head. "Think again." He cocks the hammer and holds the barrel close to Allenby's face. "Now LeSsave's done for. You're next."

Allenby smiles at him. "This way." In the courtyard, one of the candle holes, when pried, opens a flush door; steps lead down to a tiny room; Laura is on a cot, obviously drugged. Webster has Allenby carry her to the coupe, lay her on the back seat, cover her with a blanket.

"What's the drug, Allenby?"

"A sleeping herb of Caribbean derivation. She'll awaken in three or four hours with a headache. She'll be hungry, but other than that, fine."

Allenby is bending over the fallen LeSsave as Webster backs the coupe around, heads for the bungalow. You've never killed a man before, Webster. You never know what you're capable of. Was it worth it? He glances at the sleeping form behind him. Webster thinks it was.

Barton is waiting for him at the bungalow; helps carry Laura into the bedroom; waits for Webster in the living room.

"How is she?"

The Devil's Game

"Sleeping. According to Allenby, she'll come out of it in three hours or so."

"Well, that's good news."

"Yeah. Can you wait until I see how she is before you take me, Sheriff?"

Barton looks at him quizzically. "Take you?"

"I shot LeSsave."

"I know. I got a radio report that he's on the way to the hospital."

Webster shrugs. "If not for murder, for the attempt."

"Wouldn't think Allenby would want to press charges. Or LeSsave. Too many questions about why Laura was there."

Webster sits down. Stares at a wall. Hadn't quite thought it all out had you, Webster? But then why . . .

"I don't get it, Jack."

"Get what?"

"Allenby. This whole thing. What is he doing?"

Barton smiles. "Don't look at me, Webster. If you can't figure out his game, I'm sure I can't. I'm just a kind of straightforward fellow myself. All this subtlety tends to slip right by me."

"Allow me to disbelieve that, Jack."

Barton grins. "You believe what you want, Webster. It's all right with me. I've got to go over to the hospital and make sure the reports say what they need to."

"An edited version of reality."

"You might say that, but hell"—he shrugs—"that's about all we have, isn't it? Edited versions?"

Webster nods; Barton is gone; he checks on Laura who seems to sleep peacefully. Thinking about it, it occurs to Webster that by the logic of the thing, Allenby must come to see him; tonight. Why? Webster shrugs; it just seems to be the way it will go.

Webster prepares. Fire in the fireplace; box of cigars on the

The Devil and Webster Daniels

table between two easy chairs; bottle of Martel Cordon Bleu and two snifters. Not quite as elegant as Allenby did, but it will have to do, Webster.

Checks on Laura; sleeping. Sits in one of the chairs; lights a cigar; pours himself some brandy. Webster waits. The cigar is half gone and the brandy relaxing you, Webster. You feel tired and older, don't you, Webster? Attrition.

The flames rise and flicker at an influx of cold air; then relapse. Don't look around, Webster, just sit and pull on your cigar. Sip your brandy. Don't look at him as he sits down.

"I'm afraid the cognac and cigars aren't up to your standards, but you'll just have to rough it."

Allenby chuckles softly. "They're more than adequate, Webster. Very thoughtful of you." He pours himself brandy, lights a cigar. They sit in the changing light and shadow of the fire. The silence is uncomfortable, Webster.

"What's the point, Allenby?"

"I would have thought you'd have seen it by now."

"Guess I'm just a little slow tonight. You'll have to fill me in."

"Why, you've lost of course."

Webster shakes his head. "I don't see it."

"But my dear fellow, it's a contest of wills and yours failed. You don't believe in violence. You detest it. You pride yourself on winning with wit and a certain amount of second-story expertise. LeSsave will live, but you intended those shots to be fatal. You would have killed me."

"Yes."

"Assuming, of course, that I can be killed." Webster snorts. "Whether you believe that aspect of my being or not, you can't deny that your will failed."

"I don't quite see it. I'll have to think on it."

"Do so, by all means. I shall expect to hear from you. This cigar and the brandy really are quite good."

The Devil's Game

He is gone. Have you lost, Webster? You don't know, do you? You don't even know if you care. Check on Laura; you won't be able to rest until you see how she is when she awakens; Webster waits.

And when she does, she has a headache, is hungry. Webster cooks steak and eggs for her and she tells him.

"Just as I was about to get on the train in New York, a man handed me a note from you."

"From me?"

"It looked like your handwriting anyway. It said to get off at Katonah and a man in a Mercedes sedan would bring me to you. It said you would explain. So I did and this young dark man was in the sedan and said we were going to meet you."

"Harry Reynolds, maybe?"

"I don't know. He took me to a motel room and said you were in it. I went in and LeSsave and Allenby were waiting. They forced me down and injected me with something and I've been out ever since. All that time is a blank."

"How do you feel, now?"

"Not too bad. Scared, but other than that, it's just like I've had a long sleep."

"Which is what you've had. But physically, how do you feel? Your . . . body?"

"What do you mean?"

"Are you bruised? Do you feel like anything was done to you?"

She stares at him, chews slowly. "No. Why?" He explains about the phone calls. Laura stares in near disbelief, then shivers. "My God, what a swine."

Webster nods. "He's damn near got me convinced he is the devil after all."

Laura shakes her head. "No, if any of those things had been done, I'd know it. I'm sure I wasn't touched."

The Devil and Webster Daniels

"I suppose the idea is that I'm to feel even more that my will failed because I was tricked."

"You know, Webster, I'm not terribly amused by all this. I used to call myself your bishop's pawn, but that was a love joke more or less."

He sighs. "I know, love. Actually being used as a pawn isn't much of a joke. But how can you avoid being vulnerable if you love someone? Someone wanting to get at you could use me as a pawn."

"Yes. They certainly could."

He smiles. "Not that I want to be used that way, but I'm glad I'm vulnerable."

Laura kisses him on the cheek. "I guess we'll have to live with it." She finishes the breakfast. "What now?"

"I guess we'll have to ask Vera to have that dinner party. As soon as the film is ready." Laura nods.

CHAPTER VII

Beat the Devil II

False spring again in March; seventy-degree days with sun; cool evenings; attempts at vegetation and the occasional bird. Dinner party at the mansion. Vera and Caulder hosting the members of the coven and Allenby. Everyone is apprehensive; they thought they were out of it. Vera had to put the pressure on to get them all here. Everyone drinks a few too many before dinner, too much wine with dinner; bits of laughter burst, seem shrill, stop abruptly; conversation is stilted. Only Allenby seems amused and Webster is calm. After dinner, they go into the library. A screen and projector and chairs have been arranged. Webster must make a speech. Everyone is seated.

The Devil and Webster Daniels

"We've arranged for a little film we think everyone will find amusing. As you know, Satanism is something of an in thing at the moment and we are fortunate enough to have Mr. Allenby, who is a believer and practicer, with us. The film will show you something of the ritual he uses and the ceremony. We think you'll find it amusing and entertaining, if not enlightening." Lights out; the projector starts.

The courtyard at night. Allenby's voice is heard. "Light the candles." Long shot shows LeSsave lighting the candles that have been arranged in the ritual pentagram within a circle. Allenby's voice. "In the name of the fallen angels . . ." Shot of wind sputtering then extinguishing some of the candles. Front view of Allenby in his fur robes with hands on hips; his voice. "Light the candles." (A few people are giggling.) Repeat of the long shot of LeSsave lighting candles. Front view of Allenby with upraised arms. "In the name of the fallen angels . . ." Repeat shot of sputtering and dying candles. Allenby with hands on hips again. Sound track is louder so it seems he is shouting, "LIGHT THE CANDLES!" (Laughter is increasing.) Long shot shows the wolves wandering into the lighted circle. Allenby's voice. "Not now." Shot of one wolf relieving himself on a candle. Allenby: "LeSsave!" Pause. "LIGHT THE CANDLES!" (Laughter is contagious; tension, booze, heavy food make the reaction almost hysterical; even Laura and Webster are laughing hard and they have seen it before.)

With repetition, juxtaposition, and rerecorded voice-over, the film editor has made a slapstick comedy of the parts of the film that show Allenby and LeSsave and the wolves. It wouldn't draw this response in a theater, Webster, but these people are so relieved, they are laughing themselves sick; holding their sides; tears in their eyes. The film runs twenty-two minutes and finishes to sustained applause.

Lights on; look around; Allenby is gone and no one saw him slip out. Webster is smirking.

"I guess Mr. Allenby doesn't share our sense of humor. Too bad."

They are all quite relieved; loose and drinking, talking, laughing; exorcism of sorts. Webster and Laura stay as long as decency requires, not longer.

Back in the bungalow, they pack for the departure they both feel is overdue. Later, the love is fine and they feel themselves again.

In the morning, Webster calls Jack Barton to fill him in; does.

"I think that's about it, Jack. You can relax. We'll be leaving this afternoon and unless I'm way off, I think you can bet that Allenby will be leaving soon."

"Yeah, that LeSsave fellow was released from the hospital this morning. Pretty tough character."

"Yes. I guess you'll be glad to have a peaceful county again."

"Can't say I won't, but don't take it personal. I kind of like you, Webster. You and that lady of yours are sure a pair."

"I don't suppose you want that little item back. The one you loaned me the other night."

"I'd be right happy if I never laid eyes on it again. You might keep it as a souvenir."

"I guess I could do that."

"You and your lady take care, Webster."

"Hang loose, Jack."

They say their good-bys to Vera and Caulder; he looks quite relieved; they have borrowed the blueberry coupe to drive into the city. Sunny, mild March day; easy drive; back

The Devil and Webster Daniels

at the Stanhope for a few days until the ship leaves; do the town, see a few shows, feel unafraid again.

Mail at the hotel brings a large manila envelope one day. Inside, the pact on parchment and a note:

> Webster,
> Let's just call it a draw, shall we? I owe you an apology for underestimating your resources. Perhaps we will meet again and resume our little game another time.
> Edward Allenby

The Beatles; "Let It Be."

Cunard liner across the Atlantic; nine days to Southampton; first class and the off season; often seems as if they have the ship to themselves. Three days to get over the seasickness and then they start stuffing you like livestock they're readying for market; breakfast at nine with eggs, bacon, ham, roast beef, broiled tomatoes, kippers, juice, milk, coffee, tea, dry toast, fresh fruit; tea at eleven with little sandwiches and cakes; luncheon at one with cocktails, appetizers, soup, fish and meat and poultry entrees to choose from, french pastry, a cheeseboard, liqueurs; tea at four with little sandwiches and cakes; dinner at eight with seven courses and appropriate wines; midnight buffet for the late snack.

"Roll me back to the cabin and find a pin, Laura."

"Roll yourself; I can't move."

"No mercy, the woman has no mercy."

"Let's go for a walk. It'll help."

"You walk; I'm going to waddle."

Chill whippy night; coat bundlers; deck strollers. Arm in arm and the air eases the asphyxia, Webster. She wants to say something, hasn't the words.

Beat the Devil II

"I wonder if I'm making a mistake, Webster?"

"What about?"

"The magazine. Why did they hire me? What do I really know about it?"

"About as much as anybody else when they're first starting. She hired you because she was impressed with you from our interview, because you are familiar with the European scene and can speak three languages besides English."

"I just feel . . . intimidated."

"You'll do fine, Laura. You've got brains, wit, and guts. That's all you need."

"You couldn't come with me to Paris? At least for a few weeks?"

Webster shaking his head. "You've got to stop asking me that or I'll weaken. Your first instinct was right. You need to get started on your own. Make it without me or anyone else as an emotional backstop. Then when you feel secure in your independence, your working ability, then we can be together."

"Heartless."

"Nice talk. You think I want you to take off? I'd just rather have you feel whole and free when we are together. You know us, love, nothing but all the way does it."

"I know, I know. Me and my big mouth." And they've even adjusted to love-making in a moving bed.

Dock at Southampton; train to London; Hotel Rodney on Hyde Park; small and imperturbable. London shows and restaurants; few parties with old acquaintances and friends; April breaking pleasantly and see the favorite sights again; Webster never tires of the Abbey and the Tower; pretend there won't be a time to go. Make love to last.

Then the day comes and she doesn't want you to come to the airport; looks almost coltish in her yellow pants suit and dark glasses and she's almost thirty-two.

"We haven't really been apart for eight years."

The Devil and Webster Daniels

"I know."
"I'm not sure what I'll feel like."
"Me either."
"I'll call when I get in."
"You better." A long kiss, Webster, and it happens again; you could take her right here on the sidewalk with the taxi waiting. "Heathrow, driver." And the cab swings into traffic flow; her face is turned to you from the rear window.

Walking along the street, your image is slightly shopworn; that face of yours and the less-than-new belted trench coat. Crosses over and sits on a bench in Hyde Park. Clouds look like rain. Tomorrow you have to see Bobbie Deams and this mysterious friend. You're forty now, Webster. Your birthday came and went and you hardly noticed. Pretty soon, you're going to feel like a man with a past.

Paul Simon; "Papa Hobo."

DATE DUE

Smith, Terrence Lore
  The devil and Webster
Daniels
             X47203

Red Wing Public Library
Red Wing, Minnesota 55066